Rattled!

Bess and George followed me back to the tent. I crouched and unzipped the flap. Under the noise of the zipper I heard a strange sound. I paused a moment, trying to identify it. A dry rattle, like seeds in a gourd. Where was it coming from?

I shrugged and finished unzipping the tent. As the flap fell open, the sound got louder.

Zhhh-zhh-zhhh!

It was coming from inside the tent!

I looked in. I saw a raised head, coiled body, and shaking tail.

I was staring at a rattlesnake.

NANCY DREW
girl detective®

Available from Aladdin Paperbacks

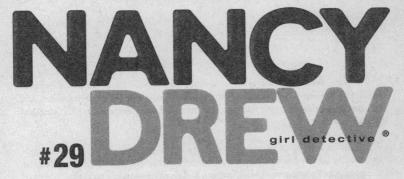

NANCY DREW

girl detective ®

#29

The Stolen Bones

CAROLYN KEENE

Aladdin Paperbacks
New York   London   Toronto   Sydney

This book is a work of fiction. Any references to historical events, real people, or real locales are used fictitiously. Other names, characters, places, and incidents are the product of the author's imagination, and any resemblance to actual events or locales or persons, living or dead, is entirely coincidental.

🐫ALADDIN PAPERBACKS

An imprint of Simon & Schuster Children's Publishing Division

1230 Avenue of the Americas, New York, NY 10020

Copyright © 2008 by Simon & Schuster, Inc.

All rights reserved, including the right of reproduction in whole or in part in any form.

NANCY DREW, NANCY DREW: GIRL DETECTIVE, ALADDIN PAPERBACKS, and related logo are registered trademarks of Simon & Schuster, Inc.

Manufactured in the United States of America

First Aladdin Paperbacks edition April 2008

10 9 8 7 6 5 4 3 2 1

Library of Congress Control Number 2007934380

ISBN-13: 978-1-4169-3614-5

ISBN-10: 1-4169-3614-9

Contents

Trespass

"What have you gotten us into now, Nancy?"

I glanced over at Bess in the front passenger seat. Her eyes were sparkling, so I knew she was only teasing me. Bess and her cousin George are my best friends, and I do get them into trouble sometimes—mostly when we're on the trail of a mystery. We weren't trying to find a criminal now, though. We were trying to find a road.

George was hunched over her GPS unit in the backseat. "Hey, we're not lost. I can tell you exactly where we are. It's the road that's lost. And if we had the GPS coordinates of the turnoff, I could tell you where *it* was too."

"I did ask," I reminded her. "They didn't know the coordinates."

George snorted. She loves gadgets of every kind, and couldn't imagine anyone not taking advantage of a useful item like a Global Positioning System. She'd been tracking our progress since we'd left River Heights two days before.

Bess pointed to our left. "There's a road. Or is it a trail? It's something, anyway."

I slowed my car and idled near the turn. The land around us was dry scrubland, with plenty of rocks and weeds, but few road signs. The rutted dirt trail on our left might have been wide enough for a car, but calling it a road seemed generous. Still, our directions said "go six miles, to the third dirt road on the left." We'd driven ten miles looking for a major dirt road, without luck, as the sun had headed for the horizon. So we'd decided that whoever had written the directions had a definition of *road* that was different from ours. We had decided to backtrack and start over.

"I guess we can try it." I turned the car and eased it onto the dirt path. Scraggly brush grew up the center, with deep ruts on either side. I kept my wheels on high ground so the bottom of my car wouldn't scrape.

"And if we don't find the place soon," Bess said cheerfully, "we can turn back to that last town and get a hotel room."

I smiled. Bess doesn't like to be away from her shower and hair dryer. I wondered if her perfectly manicured nails, painted a soft pink to match her rosy cheeks, would survive this trip.

"We're hardly roughing it," I said. "We're car camping, so you won't even have to carry a pack. We'll have our cooler right there, and even a camp cook to fix our meals."

George muttered, "Yeah, talk about roughing it. I'll be away from my computer for almost a week!"

Bess and I laughed. George must have had a dozen gadgets with her, but without her full computer setup, she acted like she was living in the Dark Ages.

"Look," I said, "this is going to be fun. How often do you get to see dinosaurs in their natural habitat?"

Bess grinned. "So long as they've been dead for a few million years, I'm happy."

George leaned forward. "I'm excited too, Nancy. We're just teasing you. I think volunteering for a paleontology dig is a great idea!"

"Thanks. I just hope we can find it." The track crossed what looked like a shallow old streambed. I eased the car forward, but it only lurched, throwing us against our seat belts.

"Uh-oh," George said. "That didn't feel good."

"No." I turned off the engine. "We'd better get out and take a look."

We opened our doors. "Ugh!" Bess said. "The ground is all muddy here."

I stepped gingerly onto the soft ground and crouched to peer under my car. "Whoops." This was a streambed all right. The last time it had rained, water must have run across our "road." The ground was wet and our front wheels had sunk into the mud. "I didn't realize the ground was so soft here. I guess I should have checked before trying to drive across."

"So how are we going to get out of here?" George asked.

The wind whipped my shoulder-length hair into my face, so I swept it into a ponytail. "I guess we should try pushing. Bess, why don't you get behind the wheel, and George and I will shove. We'd better try to go backward."

Bess slid into the driver's seat while George and I crouched in front of the car. Our feet sank into the mud. Bess put the car in reverse and gently pressed the gas while George and I leaned against the front. The car rocked slightly. But despite our grunts and groans, the only thing that moved was the mud—as the tires spun, the mud splattered all over us.

Finally George and I stood up, gasping. Bess put the car in park and got out. "We can try digging around the tires and then packing in dry sand and rocks," she said.

I glanced at the sun sinking toward the western

mountains and sighed. We didn't have much light left. "We'd better get started."

"Hey!" A loud voice startled us. "What are you girls doing?"

We turned to see a woman hurrying toward us across the field. She was in her forties, thin and wiry, with dark hair and a weather-beaten tanned face. She wore faded jeans and a denim shirt with the sleeves rolled up.

My initial relief that someone had found us faded as I noticed her scowl.

"This is private property," she yelled. "You're trespassing!"

I forced myself to smile as the woman came panting up to us. "We didn't mean to trespass," I said. "We're going on a paleontology dig, and we thought this might be the road we're supposed to take."

The scowl eased itself into a straight line. "Oh. You're one of them." She grudgingly admitted, "Yeah, this is the right track. I said them fools could go through my land. I can't understand why people would want to waste time digging up old bones, but so long as they make their mess on that government land and not on mine, I guess I don't care."

"The museum is learning more about the past," I said. "They might even discover some new species."

She snorted. "Who cares about that? It's today that matters. Ranching is real work." She looked us up and down, her eyes lingering on Bess's short skirt and sandals. "But it don't look like you girls know anything about that. I told my Jimmy that's the kind of foolishness college leads to. Better to get a real job and make some money instead of spending it on school."

I was still trying to think of a response when George said, "There is money in paleontology! Dinosaur bones can sell for millions of dollars."

The ranch woman gaped at her. "You don't say? You mean some of them bones out there might be worth millions?" She laughed. "If I'd known that, maybe I would have kept them for myself."

I glanced at the setting sun. We still had two miles to go on this road and we were running out of light. I pasted on my brightest smile. "We really are sorry to cause you any trouble, but our car is stuck. Do you have a couple of boards or something that we can stick under the wheels?"

She frowned at the car. "I guess if I want you off my property, I'll have to rescue you. Hold on a minute. I'll get my son."

She trotted away. George, Bess, and I stared at one another and simultaneously let out a long sigh of relief.

George whispered, "You sure do attract interesting people, Nan. I can't wait to meet her son."

"I just hope he hurries," I said.

We watched the sun drop behind the distant hills in a blaze of pink and gold. The temperature also dropped about ten degrees, so we retrieved our sweaters from the car. George frowned at her watch. "We have about half an hour of fading light left. Looks like we'll be setting up our tent in the dark."

At last a dirty white pickup bounced toward us. It turned and backed up so it was about ten feet in front of my car. The woman got out, along with a young man, maybe eighteen or twenty. He, too, was thin and wiry, with tangled dark hair.

I stepped closer and smiled. "Thank you for helping us. I'm Nancy Drew, by the way, and these are my friends Bess and George."

He stared at us. Like his mother, he studied Bess especially closely. I think his opinion was different, though—his eyes widened and his jaw dropped open. Bess is a natural beauty who usually looks like she just stepped out of a fashion magazine.

Bess gave him a dimpled smile and said, "Hello. Thanks for helping us out. It's really nice of you."

He only continued to stare. I started to wonder if he could even talk.

His mother stepped forward. "I'm Erlinda and this

is Jimmy. Now enough chitchat; let's get you out of here."

We weren't arguing with that! Jimmy reached into the back of the truck and pulled something out. He attached it to his truck's trailer hitch, and then pulled the other end toward my car.

"Oh, a come-along!" Bess said. "That will make things so much easier."

Jimmy paused again to stare at her, until his mother gave him a shove. He bent his head and fumbled around under my front bumper. He tightened the come-along, got back into the truck, and slowly pulled the truck forward. The car finally came out of the mud with a sucking sound. Jimmy kept going until my car was safely across the muddy area. Then he got out and unhooked the come-along as we picked our way across the mud.

"Thanks so much," I said. I wondered if I should offer money for the help. "Um, can I give you—?"

Erlinda interrupted. "You said them dinosaur bones could be worth millions of dollars? Is that true?"

"Well, I don't know about these particular bones. Fossils can sell for a lot of money, but they have to be rare to get millions." I worried that Erlinda might have ideas about scavenging the dig after the paleontologists left. "Of course, you need a special permit, like this team from the museum has. If you steal fossils, you can get big fines and jail time."

Erlinda nodded. "Oh sure, but bones on my own land, they'd be mine, right? And if there's bones just down there, maybe there's some here, too!"

"You would probably own any fossils you find on your own land," I said cautiously. "But I don't know if you'd find anything valuable. It depends on lots of things. The age of the rock, for example."

She kept nodding, but I wasn't sure whether or not she was actually listening. "Right, right. Well, just keep going down this road and you'll find them diggers."

After we thanked her, Erlinda got into the truck with Jimmy and they drove away.

"Ten minutes until dark," George said. "Let's get moving."

We did our best to scrape the mud from our shoes, and piled into my car. Everything was gray, like a faded black-and-white photo. I turned on the headlights and drove slowly along the dirt track.

George leaned over the seat back. "Well, Nancy, you've done it again."

"What are you talking about?"

"You found a mystery already," she said, laughing. "Why are these people so odd?"

I smiled. "Odd maybe, but hardly mysterious. Not everyone can be as normal as you are, George."

Bess burst out laughing. When she caught her breath, she said, "I guess we should expect people to be different here in New Mexico, anyway."

"Oh, come on," George said. "We're not in a foreign country. New Mexico is one of the fifty states, you know."

Bess twisted in her seat to poke her cousin. "I know that! But it's still going to be different from River Heights, don't you think? All this desert, and the Spanish culture."

I let them tease each other. Bess and George may be cousins, but they couldn't be more different, in everything from looks to temperament. George is tall and thin, with short dark hair and a cynical attitude. Bess is blond, shorter, and curvy, with optimism that some people would call naïve.

I guess I'm somewhere in the middle. I try to see the best in people, but I've uncovered too many criminals to think that people are nice all the time.

At that moment, driving needed my full attention. The track twisted around, and my wheels kept slipping on big rocks. I winced as a bush scraped against the side of the car. This was one place where a big truck would have been handy. I had to remind myself of all the fuel the hybrid had saved on the long drive from River Heights.

I was hunched over the wheel, clutching it tightly,

when I noticed another glow ahead, over a hill. The sun had long since vanished, and we were miles from any city. I squinted and focused on the glowing light.

I smiled, realizing what I was seeing. This mystery was easy to solve—campfire. "Hey, I think we found the camp!"

Finally we'd arrived. I put the car in park and slumped back. George bounded out of the car, and Bess and I followed her.

I'd parked among the other vehicles—trucks, SUVs, and one Land Rover. A cheerful fire sent warm light and dancing shadows over a group of people sitting in camp chairs.

A man got up and walked toward us. Bess nudged George, whispering something. Even without hearing her words, I could guess her reaction to the tall, well-built form striding toward us. We went over to meet him.

"You must be the River Heights crew," he said. "We were starting to worry about you."

"You're not the only one," George muttered.

I held out my hand. "I'm Nancy Drew. This is Bess Marvin and George Fayne."

He shook hands with each of us. "I'm Kyle, the dig leader for this trip. It's great to have you here."

"We're excited," I said. "I'm sorry we couldn't get

here earlier, but my dad needed help at his law office, and George and her mother had a big catering job to do."

"Don't worry about it," Kyle said. "We still have plenty of work to do!"

"Have you found anything interesting so far?" George asked.

Even in the dark I could see his face light up. "You bet! Our best find is still over at the dig site. We can't take it out until it's encased in plaster for protection, so you'll see that tomorrow. We also picked up some loose pieces that are really cool. Come on; I'll show you."

I glanced over at the group sitting around the fire. I was more interested in getting some food, but Kyle wanted to share his find. We followed him to the back of the Land Rover, where he pulled out a plastic tub.

As he pried off the lid, Kyle said, "These vertebrae are from a creature sort of like a crocodile—" He stopped mid-sentence and his jaw dropped open. He looked around, as if searching for someone. "Steffi!"

George, Bess, and I exchanged looks and shrugged. A petite young woman—Steffi, we assumed—strode over to us. "What's wrong?"

Kyle held out the plastic tub. It was empty. "The bones are gone!"

2

Noise in the Night

Steffi's pretty face puckered in confusion. "But I didn't move them. I labeled them, wrapped them in paper towels, and put them in the box."

Kyle looked worried. "And you brought the box back to camp yourself?"

Steffi shook her head. "Tom carried it back to camp for me." She ran her hand through her short dark hair and, without turning around, called, "Tom!"

A young man walked toward us. "Something wrong?"

Kyle and the woman turned to him. "Where are the bones we found yesterday?"

He glanced at the open tub Kyle still held. "I have no idea. You mean they're not there?" His face went hard. "You're not suggesting I—"

"No, no," Kyle said quickly. "We just wondered if you took them out to study them or something." He looked at us and seemed to suddenly remember that three strangers were witnessing their exchange. "I'm sorry. This isn't much of a welcome for you."

"That's all right," I said. "If something's wrong, we'd like to help."

Kyle shrugged. "I'm sure it's nothing. The bones will turn up." His unhappy face didn't match his confident words.

Steffi smiled at us and held out her hand. "Hi. I'm Steffi." She barely came up to my shoulder but she had a strong handshake and moved like a gymnast.

"Steffi is my assistant here," Kyle said.

"You're a paleontologist?" I asked. She looked only a couple of years older than us.

"I'm a student, working toward my master's degree. So is Tom."

The young man managed a smile and shook hands. He was medium height and medium build, with brown hair and tan skin. Bess glanced between him and Kyle, and I could almost see her mind working. Tom wasn't bad-looking, but Kyle was definitely Bess's type, with close-cropped blond hair and a strong jaw. I smiled. Bess could have her pick; I was perfectly happy with my boyfriend Ned back home.

Kyle turned toward the fire. "Come meet the rest of the team."

We joined the cozy circle. A man shifted with a groan, getting ready to rise. I said, "Please, you don't have to get up. You must have all had a long day."

"Thanks," the man said. "I think my leg muscles have seized up. Kyle, next time why don't you get a hot tub out here?"

Kyle smiled. "That's Grayson. This is his first time with us."

"Hi, Grayson," I said. He was an older man, with white hair, but he looked like he was in pretty good shape despite his complaints.

The woman next to him gave a small wave. She was about forty, with silvery blond hair that hung over her shoulder in a thick braid. "I'm Abby. They'll tell you I'm the flaky one."

"We've never said that," Grayson protested. "At least not within your range of hearing!"

Abby just laughed. "Don't worry; I'm used to it."

"I'm Russell," the next man said. He was probably in his fifties, with a stocky build and a thick brown beard. "Just another volunteer here. I've gone on these digs all around the country, but this is my first time with this group."

"Russell really knows his bones," Kyle said. "Some

15

of our volunteers know more than Steffi and I do. And that brings us to Felix."

The last one of the group stood up, despite my protest. He was easily the oldest person there, perhaps over seventy, with hunched shoulders but a firm handshake.

"Felix has been coming to these digs for almost forty years," Kyle said. "What he doesn't know about fossils probably isn't worth knowing."

"I don't have any formal training," Felix said. "I'm just an interested amateur, but I've been around a long time. Unfortunately, I can't dig anymore, with my bad heart. But they let me come along anyway. Now I'm the camp cook." He grinned around at all of us. "Speaking of which, who's ready for dinner?"

Bess, George, and I had gotten a warm enough welcome, but everyone greeted food with cheers. Felix dished out sloppy joes, the thick meat sauce spilling over hamburger buns. Steffi offered sodas from a big cooler. Then she and Kyle sat together on the cooler and gave us their chairs. Tom insisted that Bess take his chair, and he sat cross-legged on the ground.

"This place is dangerous," Bess said, eyeing her plate. She usually tries to be careful about what she eats.

George shoveled food into her mouth. "You'll work it off tomorrow."

Steffi laughed. "It's not health food, but after a long day of work, nothing beats Felix's culinary creations. We're lucky. On most digs the volunteers have to bring and fix their own food. This is a real treat!"

Felix gave a dismissive wave. "So who's ready for seconds?"

I was stuffed after firsts, but everyone who'd been working that day went back for more. I studied their faces, reminding myself of the names. It seemed like a nice bunch, and they teased one another like old friends. Even the first-timers had had two days to get to know each other.

When everyone was finished, we burned the paper plates in the fire. Felix washed the silverware in a little water from a bucket. The bottles and soda cans went into special bags for recycling later.

It was still pretty early, but people started drifting off to their tents.

George stretched and yawned. "You guys ready? We still have a tent to set up."

Bess made a face. "I'd forgotten."

"At least we'll be able to see by the moon," George said. "It's full tonight."

"How do you know?" I asked. George picks up all kinds of trivia on the Internet, so I figured she'd checked a site with moon data.

"It's rising right over there."

I turned. A huge golden moon seemed to float above the eastern horizon. "Wow. It's beautiful!"

We watched for a minute. Out of the corner of my eye, I saw a flicker a movement. When I turned, I saw Steffi and Kyle heading back to the Land Rover and poking around in the back. "Just a minute," I told my friends. "I want to ask Steffi and Kyle about those bones again. Something tells me they're more concerned than they're letting on."

When I reached them, Steffi turned with a small plastic tub in her arms. "These will be safe, anyway. I'll keep them in my tent tonight." She gave me a smile and walked off.

"Oh, hi," Kyle said. "Do you need something?"

"I just wanted to ask about these missing bones," I said. "Were they something important?"

"We had some very nice phytosaur vertebrae. Not the most important thing we found, but good specimens."

"Valuable?"

"Sure, but—" His eyes darted around at the people entering their tents. "No one here would take them. It has to be an accident."

Steffi must disagree, I thought, if she was taking the other fossils to bed with her. "Is fossil theft a big problem?"

Kyle scowled. "You wouldn't believe it. People

pull off some pretty brazen thefts. There's been a rash of them in the Southwest lately—" He stopped suddenly. "It's nothing for you to worry about. It's perfectly safe here. I promise."

"I wasn't worried about our safety—"

He cut me off. "You had a long drive today. Get some sleep." He put a hand on my arm to turn me away.

I sighed and left him to close up the Land Rover. I could ask more questions in the morning, when we were both rested.

I joined Bess and George. "Anything interesting?" George whispered.

I shrugged. "I didn't get much information. Kyle probably doesn't want to sound suspicious of his volunteers. But from the way he and Steffi are acting, I'd say the bones were stolen, not just lost. Keep your eyes open tomorrow."

Bess grinned. "So you found a real mystery after all. And if you don't count the long drive out here, it came up within the first five minutes of our vacation. This may be a record."

I laughed along with their good-natured teasing. We got our tent and flashlights from the car and scouted out a flat place. It didn't take long to put up the tent.

At home I can be ready for bed in ten minutes.

Out there it took more like half an hour. We had to find everything in our luggage, brush our teeth with bottled water, and trot off into the darkness to go to the bathroom. Finally we settled down in our sleeping bags. I shivered despite my flannel pajamas, and snuggled deeper.

"Should I set an alarm?" Bess asked.

George groaned.

"I expect we'll hear everyone else getting up," I said.

"Still, I could set one just to be safe," Bess offered.

"No thanks!" George said. "Besides, we don't even know what time they want to start."

I tried to change the subject. "This is kind of like a slumber party."

Bess giggled. "Who brought the popcorn?"

George said, "If I had my laptop, we could watch movies."

"We could watch one movie, before the batteries ran out." I yawned. "Anyway, I'm tired, and it sounds like we're going to be working hard tomorrow."

They mumbled their agreement. The night was filled with the chirping of crickets. It was hardly quiet, but made a nice change from city noises. I felt myself sinking into sleep.

Until someone screamed.

3

Footprints in the Dark

I tried to jump up, but I hit my head on the tent and stumbled in my sleeping bag. I collapsed back. Bess squealed and pushed me off of her. I fumbled for my sleeping bag zipper, but by that point I was tangled and disoriented. I started wiggling out the top.

A light flashed in my face. It danced around the tent, then settled as George hooked a big flashlight to a loop in the roof.

"That was a scream, right?" George asked.

"That was me," Bess said. "Nancy sat on me."

I shoved my sleeping bag aside and unzipped the tent. "Before that. Someone definitely screamed out there." I found my shoes just outside the tent and slid my feet into them.

George and I crawled out of the tent together.

21

Someone ran past, and I thought I recognized Kyle.

"Kyle!" I called. "What's going on?"

He yelled, "That was Steffi," and kept running.

George and I followed, stumbling in the darkness. It was a good thing Kyle knew where Steffi had pitched her tent. She was pretty far from the camp, hidden between a rock outcropping and one of the few small trees. She was crouched in the tent opening when we arrived.

Kyle knelt in front of her and took her arms. "Are you all right?"

"I'm fine." She sounded perfectly calm. "I'm sorry I startled you."

"You scared me half to death!" Kyle exclaimed. "What happened?"

A light came bobbing up, and I turned to see Bess. Somehow she'd managed to get fully dressed. She handed George and me our coats and we pulled them on gratefully.

Tom and Russell jogged over from the campsite. Grayson trailed behind them. We were missing only Abby and Felix. Maybe they'd slept through the noise.

Steffi stood up. "I'm sorry I frightened everyone. I heard noises outside my tent. Probably just an animal."

Kyle said, "But you've never—"

Steffi shot him a look and he closed his mouth.

22

Bess wedged herself between George and me and shone the flashlight into the shadows. "What kind of animals do you have here? Anything dangerous?"

"Not really," Steffi said. "Just rabbits, possums, skunk, maybe deer or coyote."

Bess's light jerked. "Coyote?"

Steffi laughed. "I've never heard of them attacking a person. Now why don't you all go back to bed?"

Russell and Tom headed back toward camp. Grayson said, "Save the next wake-up call for nine a.m.," and gave us a friendly grin as he passed.

"Do you really think it could have been a coyote?" Bess whispered. "Maybe I'll sleep in the car."

"Probably just a rabbit," I said, to comfort her. "Let me see the flashlight." I examined the ground around Steffi's tent. I saw tracks all right, but they weren't animal tracks. I found human footprints, with the thick heel and pointed toe of cowboy boots. They came from the direction of the road, toward the tent, and away again. The return tracks were deeper at the toes, and farther apart, as if the person had been running. And they looked fresh. The wind that afternoon would surely have softened the edges more.

I put my foot next to the track. The footprint was much longer, probably a man's. I glanced at Kyle's heavy hiking boots.

He was watching me, and must have seen what I

23

saw, but he didn't say anything. Steffi spoke sharply. "I said everything's fine. Why don't you go back to bed?"

Steffi didn't sound scared—more like angry. Was she just embarrassed because she had screamed? She didn't seem like the type who would scream for no reason. But if a man was sneaking around her tent at night, maybe she should be scared. "Steffi, someone was here," I said. "A man. Don't you think it would be safer to move your tent closer to the others?

Her teeth flashed in the moonlight. "Don't worry about me. I can take care of myself."

Kyle said, "Thanks for your help. I'll stay with Steffi for a while. You'd better get back to bed."

They obviously wanted to get rid of us, and I was feeling the cold despite my coat. I handed the flashlight back to Bess, and she led the way to our tent. We didn't speak until we were tucked away inside.

"Nancy, what did you get us into?" Bess said. "I'm sure you didn't mention coyotes."

"Coyotes aren't what's worrying me." I filled them in on the tracks I'd seen.

"Who could it be?" Bess said. "We're in the middle of nowhere."

"Exactly," I said. "As far as we know, there are only nine people besides us within a few miles of here."

George counted on her fingers. "Kyle, Steffi, and

five other volunteers. That means you're counting Jimmy and Erlinda?"

"Yes. Of course, we don't know if anybody else lives with them. If not, the tracks had to be Jimmy's."

"I knew he was creepy," George said. "But what about Steffi's reaction? Either she didn't know it was him, or she doesn't care."

"What do you suppose it means?" Bess asked.

I could feel my sixth sense tingling. "I don't know, but add this to the missing bones, and I have a feeling we're going to have an interesting couple of days ahead of us!"

I awoke to the sun shining through the blue nylon of the tent. I blinked a few times in the strange light before realizing where I was. My sleeping bag was warm enough, but the air on my face felt cold. From outside I heard voices and the slam of a car door.

George groaned. "What time is it?"

"Almost six o'clock," Bess said. "I told you we should have set an alarm."

George grumbled something and snuggled deeper into her sleeping bag.

I yawned and stretched. "I guess they want to start before it gets too hot."

"So they start when it's too cold?" George said. "Come back for me in an hour."

"You'll miss breakfast," Bess said. She was already sifting through her clothes. I wriggled into my clothes, then ran a brush through my hair and pulled it into a ponytail.

George sat up with a sigh. "All right, I'm awake."

"I guess it's too cold for shorts," Bess said.

"We're going to be out in the sun all day," George said. "Wear long pants and long sleeves." She frowned at Bess's pale skin. "And I hope you brought a sun hat. Sunscreen alone isn't going to do it for a full day."

Bess pouted prettily. "You take all the fun out of getting dressed."

I grinned at her. "Don't worry. I'm sure Kyle will notice you no matter what you wear."

She grinned back. "All right, you win." Somehow she still managed to look great, in tan pants and a long-sleeved white shirt, with her blond hair curling over her shoulders. George's short hair was tousled, and I avoided looking in a mirror. But leave it to Bess—even without a shower she could look like a model from an outdoors catalogue.

We shrugged into our coats and started toward the fire. I glanced around. "Steffi isn't here yet. I think I'll check on her." Bess and George nodded and went forward while I turned back. I didn't want to be a pest, but I knew I'd feel better after making sure Steffi was fine.

I managed to find the path we had taken during the night. In a few minutes I saw Steffi's tent. She was standing outside, talking to a man. It took me a minute, but I finally recognized who it was—Jimmy!

I hesitated and pulled back behind a small tree. I didn't want to interrupt, and I didn't really want to spy on them. I decided I'd just wait a minute to make sure Steffi had everything under control.

Jimmy was staring at his feet. Steffi smiled and put a hand on his arm. If anything, it looked like she was comforting him. I shook my head. It was none of my business, so long as everyone was safe.

I started to back up, but as I did, I tripped on a rock and tumbled to the ground. When I got up, Jimmy was running off and Steffi was heading toward me. I brushed myself off and gave her an embarrassed smile. "Good morning."

"Out for a morning stroll?" she asked.

I nodded. "I think breakfast is about ready, though, so I'm turning back."

"I'll join you."

As we walked back to camp, I asked, "Did you sleep well?"

"Like a log."

"No more disturbances, then?"

"A perfectly quiet night."

We went the rest of the way without speaking. I

27

still wondered about Jimmy, but I gathered the pale-ontologists had been working at the site for a couple of years, so it made sense that he knew Steffi. Perhaps he even had a crush on her. His mother wouldn't like that, so it would explain why he had to sneak around. But I remembered the missing bones as well. Surely anyone sneaking around camp had to be considered suspicious. And Steffi had said she was keeping some bones in her tent last night. But if Jimmy had come after the bones, Steffi would have raised the alarm.

I shook my head to clear it. I didn't have enough to work on yet. I'd keep my eyes and ears open, and see what happened.

Felix waved a spatula as we approached. "Just in time! How does hash and eggs sound?"

"Great!" Steffi said. "And do I smell coffee?" She jogged over to Felix. He had a four-burner camp stove set up on the tailgate of a truck.

"I'll take anything warm," I said. George handed me a mug of steaming coffee and I thanked her.

Tom was stirring up the fire and adding sticks. He grinned up at me. "I just love the smell of piñon wood burning." I inhaled deeply, and had to agree.

Kyle was sorting through some gear. I heard him mutter, "That's funny. I thought we had another one of these."

Grayson crawled out of his tent and came to stand

near the fire. In daylight I realized his hair wasn't actually white, but rather a very light blond. He probably wasn't over fifty. He sniffled, pulled out a huge handkerchief, and blew his nose. He saw me watching and said, "Apparently I'm allergic to fresh air."

I heard a clatter of loose rocks and turned to see Russell slithering down a hillside. He too came to huddle over the fire. "Brr. It's windy up there, but the only place I can get cell phone reception is at the top of that hill."

"You can get cell phone reception here?" George poked me. "See, Nancy, I told you I'd want my PDA."

"Great," Bess said with a yawn. "Now you can stand on a hill in the wind and check your e-mail."

"Exactly!"

We were still missing one person. I decided Abby must be a heavy sleeper, if she could ignore Steffi's scream and now all the morning activity. Then she appeared from behind Russell's hill. Her face looked pinched with cold, but she gave us a serene smile. I noticed her eyes were an unusual color, almost violet.

Felix hurried over to her with a mug. "Up early again? You look frozen. Here's your green tea." He winked at her. "Organic, of course."

"Thank you," Abby said. "I don't feel the day has started properly unless I can do my sunrise rituals."

"Rituals?" I asked.

"Rhythmic chanting and dancing to greet the new day. I have to align my chakras with the earth's energy zones."

"Oh, I see." Actually, I didn't, but I wasn't sure getting her to explain further would help.

Abby sipped her tea. "It's so peaceful being out in the desert alone, and these ancient sites have a special spirituality."

Russell said, "You know, we're digging up dinosaur bones. There were no humans here. This isn't one of your mystical what–do–you–call–its, where your ancestors came to chant and beat drums. If your ancestors ever touched this continent, which I doubt."

Abby gave him a disapproving look. "We all came from the same mother, thousands of years ago. And all creatures can offer a spiritual connection to the earth. Humans aren't the center of everything."

I decided to break in before an argument could start. "So, what do you do, Abby? I mean, as a job?"

She turned to me, her smile serene again. "I have a little shop in Arizona. I sell jewelry and semiprecious stones with special powers." She pulled the necklace from her coat collar to show me. The smooth stone had shimmering bands of brown and yellow. A piece of silver wire held it on a leather thong. "Tiger's-eye helps focus the mind, and it offers protection during travel. I thought it the perfect stone for this trip."

"Well, it's very pretty," I said.

Bess joined us and admired the stone. "If it offers protection, you should get one, Nancy!"

Abby's eyebrows went up. "Oh? Do you need protection?"

Bess laughed. "Nancy has a habit of getting in trouble. She's an amateur detective."

Abby studied me curiously. I shrugged and said, "I've had a little luck."

"Breakfast!" Felix shouted. "Come and get it!"

The hot food tasted wonderful. I noticed that Abby wasn't eating the hash and eggs. She saw me eyeing her bowl and said, "Barley and tofu, with a bit of seaweed. I keep a macrobiotic diet. You can't be one with the world if you feast upon nature's creatures."

I gave her a noncommittal smile. By the time we'd finished breakfast, cleaned up, and brushed our teeth, the sun had warmed things up. We shed our coats and grabbed our backpacks.

"Everyone have plenty of water?" Kyle asked. "We're going about a mile from camp, so be sure to bring enough to last until lunchtime."

George had already checked our supplies of water, sunscreen, and insect repellent. We also had our big floppy hats. "We're all set. What's that stuff?"

Tom and Russell each picked up a covered five

gallon bucket. Kyle took one in each hand. Steffi and Grayson grabbed large packages.

"This is plaster," Steffi said. "And that's the water we mix into it. We cover the fossils with plaster so we can move them without damaging them."

"I'll take one," George said. She hefted a bag.

"That's enough plaster, then," Steffi said. She smiled at Bess and me. "Maybe you two can take another bucket between you?"

I picked up a bucket. It was heavy. Bess grasped the handle too, and we carried the bucket hanging between us.

I glanced back and saw Abby trailing behind us. She wasn't carrying anything except her own small backpack. I guess the tiger's-eye offered some kind of protection after all!

The ground was rough, so I was glad for my sturdy hiking boots. By the time we got to the site, I was breathless and sweating. We put the bucket down, and I shook out my aching arm. Russell sat down on his bucket with a hearty sigh. Grayson mopped sweat from his forehead. Tom and Steffi, on the other hand, were already sorting out equipment. Kyle looked like he hadn't even broken a sweat. I guess they were used to this.

George dropped off her bag of plaster and joined

us, smiling broadly. "What a great day!" She checked something on her watch. "Sixty-eight degrees already, and it's only seven thirty. Going to be a hot one." She pulled her digital camera out of her backpack and took a few shots of the scenery as the sun blazed over a ridge.

We were down in a kind of hollow, with ten-foot-high rocky cliffs around us, except for an open passage on each end. Several blue plastic tarps were spread out on the ground and weighted with rocks in the corners.

"All right," Kyle said. "Most of you can keep going from yesterday. I'll give our new guests the tour." He smiled at us. "Then we'll put you to work as well."

"We're ready," I said

"First let me show you our great find." He walked over to one of the blue tarps. Grayson was standing next to it, taking a drink from his water bottle. Abby sat on the ground nearby, cross-legged, eyes closed. It took me a moment to realize that the soft humming sound I heard was coming from her.

Kyle removed a couple of the rocks to free the tarp. He pulled it back with a flourish like a magician. "And here we have—"

He broke off with a gasp. "Oh, no!"

4

Damaged

I glanced from his astonished face to where he was staring. The ground was torn up, where someone had obviously been digging around a two-foot-square mound of gray rock. I couldn't see anything obviously wrong, but the other volunteers were gathering around with cries of dismay. Even Abby had opened her eyes and stood, peering over Grayson's shoulder.

Kyle knelt next to the pile of rocks and muttered under his breath.

I crouched next to him. "What's wrong?"

"Someone or something has been at the fossil!"

I frowned at the pile, trying to make sense of it. I thought I could see the end of a few bones. But the bones were dark gray like the rest of the rock, and the whole thing was one solid block. You could never pull out a single bone.

Kyle ran his hand over one end of the rock, where a few chisel marks showed a fresh break. "We had a beautiful jawbone right here. You could see the teeth. And now it's gone."

"You mean stolen?" I asked.

Kyle sat back on his heels and looked around at the volunteers. They stared back at him.

"Could an animal have done it?" Bess asked.

Tom moved closer to her and said softly, "Those bones are millions of years old. There's no meat on them, nothing an animal would want. They're just rock."

I thought of the missing fossils last night and looked around at the faces, wondering if one of them could be the thief. They all seemed like nice people, but who else would be out here?

Kyle stood up. "All right. Let's get to work. We need to get this fossil jacketed." He strode away, scowling.

George, Bess, and I exchanged glances. We joined Kyle by the equipment pile.

"Kyle?" I said. "Can we help somehow?"

He managed a smile. "I'm sorry, Nancy. I guess it seems like a lot of fuss. But that's the most important fossil here. It's the reason we came back this year. We found it on our last day last summer. We couldn't stay any extra days to get it out, so we covered it up. I've been looking forward to getting it all year."

"What's so special about it?" George asked.

"It's a Coelophysis, a small predatory dinosaur. It's rare to find more than a few bones. Usually after a dinosaur died, its bones were scattered—maybe scavengers carried off pieces, or a river washed some bones away. But this set looked fairly complete, from what we could see. It would have been a real treasure for the museum."

"Or anyone else," I said. I was thinking of Jimmy and Erlinda.

Kyle sighed. "Look, I want you guys to have a good time. Don't worry about this."

"Solving crimes is our idea of a good time," George said. "Nancy is an amateur detective."

Kyle's eyebrows went up. "Really?" He glanced around at the other volunteers. They were all hard at work, but he lowered his voice anyway. "I don't know what you could do, except maybe keep your eyes open. You may not realize it, but fossils are worth a lot of money on the black market."

"Last night you said something about a rash of thefts around here," I said.

"I'd guess that hundreds of fossils get stolen every year," Kyle said. "Most we never even know about. Sometimes you see them for sale on the Internet.

People claim they came from private land, but you have to wonder. Then in the last year, I've heard reports of thefts from digs and storage facilities in the Four Corners area—New Mexico, Colorado, Arizona, and Utah."

"Have you had fossils stolen at this site?" Bess asked.

"I don't think so," Kyle said, "but it's always a worry. We try to keep the site location pretty secret, but of course we have to tell the volunteers. We never have money for a full professional dig, so we depend on volunteers. And that means you more or less take whoever you get."

He shrugged and gave us a sheepish grin, as if just remembering that we were volunteers too.

"Who else knows?" I asked.

"If we need access through private land, we have to tell the landowner. People on the museum staff know. And we report on our digs through the museum website and newsletter. We only name the general location, but it's possible someone could use that to track us down, or even follow us out here. I think last year's report mentioned finding this fossil."

"So anyone could find out if they really wanted to," I said.

"Yes, I guess so," Kyle said. "Usually it doesn't matter too much. The fossils we find are good and important for the museum collection, but they're not that rare or valuable. I hate the idea of thieves making money off of them, but it's not a huge loss."

I glanced back at the spot where Steffi, Abby, and Grayson were working on the fossil. "But that one *is* rare?"

"Yes." Kyle stared at them, his jaw set. "That's why we're going to keep it safe, no matter what."

Bess put a hand on Kyle's arm. "If you have thieves around here, we'll find them!"

"Kyle, how about giving us that tour," I said. "How big is the site?"

He gestured around the hollow, which was perhaps twenty feet by forty feet. "Basically what you see here." He stepped over to the cliff wall, and we gathered around him. We could see bands in the rock, like layers in a cake. The bands had different colors, from pale tan to dark brown to reddish. In some bands the rock looked hard; in others, crumbly.

Kyle said, "Most dinosaur fossils are found in sedimentary rocks, like this. Sedimentary rocks are made up of sediments such as sand, gravel, mud, or clay. They're usually deposited in bodies of water."

Bess looked around. "So what are they doing here in the desert?"

Kyle grinned at her. "It wasn't always a desert." He gestured across the hollow. "This used to be a river, millions of years ago. Ancient rivers are a good place to find fossils, because the mud covers bones quickly. If something dies out in the desert, its bones might be scattered, or just decay. The river mud protects the bones, so they're still here for us to find. Plus, this hollow is still a river during flood season. That helps us because the water washes away the soil and exposes new things."

We walked in a circle around the site. I scanned the ground for footprints or dropped objects, but I didn't see anything out of the ordinary. With so many people wandering around the site, I probably couldn't have identified the thief's footprints anyway.

While Kyle was explaining some paleontology facts to Bess, George whispered to me, "What do you think? Jimmy?"

I frowned. "He's the most suspicious person we've met so far. But what about those missing fossils last night? If Jimmy and Erlinda had learned how valuable fossils are only when we told them, they wouldn't have had time to steal those."

"But they might have already known. Erlinda could have been putting on an act. Or Jimmy might have known, even if she didn't."

I nodded. "They're definitely suspects, but I don't want to jump to conclusions. I don't see any cowboy boot tracks here, like the ones last night. Everyone on the dig is wearing hiking boots."

Kyle turned to us. "Any more questions? I really should get to work. Our priority now is to get that fossil out."

"How long will that take?" I asked.

"Unfortunately, it won't be ready today. After we expose the top, we plaster over one side of the fossil, and let the plaster dry. Then we chisel out under the base and flip over the whole thing. We plaster the top side, and once that dries, it's ready to make the trip back to the museum, safe in its armor. It's called jacketing. We'll start plastering soon, but with the drying time it won't be ready until tomorrow. So, do you want to start with excavating or with jacketing?"

"Excavating," George said promptly. "That sounds more exciting."

"I guess I'll try jacketing," Bess said.

I pondered. It was tempting to head back to camp and poke around. But what would I look for? A smart thief would simply drop the stolen fossils under a bush until he was ready to leave, and I couldn't search the whole desert. A thief wouldn't need any special tools, either, because they were all at the site. Maybe the best thing I could do was work, ask questions, and keep an eye on everything. "Just put me wherever you need me."

"Good," Kyle said. "Bess, you can work with Steffi. They should be about ready to cover that fossil, and you couldn't learn from a better plasterer."

"Sounds good." She walked over to Steffi and Grayson.

"What happened to Abby?" I asked.

Kyle glanced around. "I guess she's gone on another one of her spiritual walkabouts or whatever she calls them. The woman is useless." He grinned at me. "Sorry. I shouldn't be so blunt."

I smiled back. "That's all right. With volunteers you have to take what you get."

"Too true. But Abby actually knows her fossils. She just doesn't want to do any work. So why on earth did she bother to come?" He sighed. "In any case, why don't you two work with Tom and Russell. Since you're the newcomers, you can split up and pair off with them."

I wound up with Tom, while George worked with Russell about ten feet away. Tom said, "This was an aetosaur we call *Typothorax*. Aetosaurs were weird plant-eating reptiles. The bones are jumbled together, so it probably died at the edge of the river, and the water carried some bones away and dumped others here. You want to get as close to the bone as possible, but you don't want to damage the fossil."

I ran my hand over a section. "How do you tell? The whole thing feels like solid stone."

"Well, that's basically what a fossil is. Minerals seep

into the bones and turn them to stone. But it's different from the surrounding area, so the rock will tend to come away."

I picked up a hammer and chisel. "So pound away until I find bone?"

"Right. We're not trying to get the bones out individually, of course. We just want to get as much rock as possible off of the top before we jacket it."

"Why? Wouldn't it be safer to just plaster the whole thing?"

"Safer, maybe, but not easier," Tom said. "Most of these jackets weigh between fifty and two hundred pounds, and big ones will weigh more. Extra rock means extra weight."

I gaped at him. "But we're a mile from the cars!"

"Yup. It's the fun part." He grinned at me. "We put the heaviest jackets on a big rescue sled and drag it. But believe me, that's no walk in the park, especially with uneven ground. And smaller fossils just go into our backpacks. Excavating is the easy part."

"I guess I'd better get busy, then." I picked up a chisel and started tapping at the rock. At first I tried to be delicate, but nothing happened. I had to tap hard to break up the rock at all.

Tom worked quickly and confidently, brushing away loose rock chips with a wide paintbrush. I thought about what he'd said. Stealing fossils wasn't like stealing jewelry. You had to know what you were doing to identify and retrieve valuable fossils. That meant the thief was an expert in the field.

Could the thief even be a paleontologist? Paleontology was a lot of work, and probably didn't pay well. "What's it like being a paleontologist?" I asked Tom.

"It's the best job in the world," he said. "At least, if you can get a job."

"Is it hard to find a job as a paleontologist?"

He sat back and wiped his face with a bandanna. "There aren't a lot of jobs. Take the museum here. Most of the staff is young, and far from retirement. And if a position does open up, you can bet that Kyle will make sure Steffi gets it."

His gaze settled on Steffi. She was dipping strips of burlap into the thick white plaster and laying them over the corner of the damaged rock. I couldn't read Tom's expression.

He went on. "But one major find can make you famous. Then you're in *National Geographic*, lecturing at museums around the world, in demand everywhere."

I studied him. He wasn't bad-looking, but his mouth turned down at the edges, and he was already getting frown lines between his eyebrows. "Is that what you want? Fame?"

"Doesn't everyone?"

"So how do you get there?"

He sighed. "My best hope is to find something that will make for a great graduate project and get me some attention. That can lead to future funding."

He lapsed into silence, and I studied him surreptitiously as we worked. Could *Tom* have a motive? Maybe he wanted to steal the fossil so he could claim he found it somewhere else and get the recognition he seems to want so badly. Could I be working side by side with a thief?

5

More Mysteries

I had a hard time concentrating on the fossil, with all the questions in my head. Plus, it kept getting hotter. But I didn't want to damage the bone by being careless. I was trying to help Kyle, not cause more problems.

Conversation died off across the site. All I could hear was the clink of tools, the buzzing of insects, and the shuffling sounds of people changing their positions. The sun beat down on us, and I wiped my face on my sleeve.

"All right, gang," Kyle called out. "Lunchtime!"

Cheers erupted in the hollow. We got to our feet and stretched. George looked at her watch and said, "Ninety-two degrees."

45

I joined Bess, who was wiping wet plaster off her hands. "Do you feel up to using your natural charm?" I whispered.

She grinned. "Always."

"Walk with Tom," I said. "It sounds like he's jealous of Steffi, and Kyle is on Steffi's side. I'd like to know if there's anything there, but he might get suspicious if I keep asking questions."

She saluted. "Agent Bess is on the case."

I dropped back behind the group as we walked, pondering other suspects. What about Jimmy and his mother? Had our meeting last night given them the idea of stealing fossils? Or had they already been at work?

Steffi was a mystery all by herself. She was smart and strong and tough. My instinct was to like her. But what about the confusion last night? Why had she pitched her tent so far from everyone else? And why would she be having secret conversations with Jimmy, if that was the case? She must have been surprised when he appeared last night, or she wouldn't have screamed. But then she acted like nothing had happened.

I didn't know much about the other people in the group. I'd have to fix that. And of course, it might not be anyone in the group at all. But with fossils missing

46

from the Land Rover as well as the dig site, a passing stranger seemed unlikely. Only someone close by would know where to find everything.

I shook my head, trying to clear it.

When I looked around, I realized I had no idea where I was.

George said, "Um, Nancy, I think we're supposed to go this way."

"Huh? Oh, right." It's a good thing I have my friends to keep me on track while I'm distracted by a mystery. Otherwise I might wind up lost in the desert!

Back at camp Felix greeted us with a smile and a cooler filled with cold drinks. The icy lemon-lime soda coursed down my throat and knocked all other thoughts from my head.

I drank about half the can, then looked at Bess and smiled. "Some morning, huh?"

She nodded and took another sip of her soda. Even in the shade of her sun hat, her cheeks looked pink. Damp tendrils of hair curled around her ears. "It was fun."

George bounded over to us, full of energy as usual. "Learn anything?" she asked, raising her eyebrows.

I shook my head. "Lots of questions, but no answers."

Bess leaned closer and lowered her voice. "I think you're right about Tom, Kyle, and Steffi. I don't think it's a love triangle. More like professional jealousy. That guy sure knows how to complain."

"I'll tackle him again this afternoon," I said. "But first let's get some lunch!"

Felix had sandwiches ready to go, piled high with meat, cheese, and vegetables. "Are you sure you don't want one?" he asked Abby. "I have a vegetarian." It looked delicious, with roasted red peppers and sprouts spilling out the sides.

She wrinkled her nose. "Thank you, but I'll stick with my herbed soybeans and millet."

Grayson picked up a sandwich stuffed with roast beef. "Ah, here's one just the way I like it—plenty of cow!"

Abby stuck her tongue out at him, and he laughed.

We got our sandwiches and looked around for shade. Tom and Russell sat under a blue tarp stretched between two trucks, talking seriously. I caught a few words, and it sounded like a foreign language. Dinosaur names, I guessed. Abby perched nearby, eating delicately like a cat. Grayson slumped against a tree, looking wilted. Steffi headed toward her tent. Felix sat by his sandwiches, ready to offer more.

Kyle looked tired, with his shoulders drooping, but he smiled and came over to us. "We usually take a couple of hours' break now. We try to head back to the dig around three o'clock. That way we avoid the worst of the heat, but still get in several more hours of work."

"Why do you do the dig when it's so hot, anyway?" George asked. "Why not wait until cooler weather?"

"A lot of our volunteers are students or teachers, so we wait for summer break."

We lapsed into silence as we finished our sandwiches. The air shimmered with heat. I felt like I was melting, and my eyes wanted to close. Soon people headed to their tents. I hesitated, feeling like I should be doing some detective work. But for the moment everyone was safely tucked away. I decided to lie down for a few minutes and then come out to keep an eye on things.

Bess and George followed me back to the tent. I crouched and unzipped the flap. Under the noise of the zipper I heard a strange sound. I paused a moment, trying to identify it. A dry rattle, like seeds in a gourd. Where was it coming from?

I shrugged and finished unzipping the tent. As the flap fell open, the sound got louder.

Zhhh-zhh-zhhh!

It was coming from inside the tent!

I looked in. I saw a raised head, coiled body, and shaking tail.

I was staring at a rattlesnake.

Rattled

6

My breath stopped while my heart raced. I couldn't move, even though I felt the adrenaline surging through my bent legs.

Behind me Bess stepped closer. "What's that noise?"

"Get back!" I croaked. I sensed rather than saw George grab Bess and the two of them carefully retreat.

The rattler had to be at least three feet long, and two inches thick. It lay smack on the middle sleeping bag, coiled up, with its head and tail raised. I stared into its unblinking eyes. Its tongue flicked in and out. Every few seconds it paused in its rattling, then started up again, the tail tip a blur.

Chills ran up and down my spine and sweat poured

down my face. I took a shallow breath and reached one hand behind me. Slowly I shifted back until I was sitting on the ground. I inched my way back, making no sudden movements, though my pounding heart was telling me to leap up and run.

The rattler shifted and slithered a little closer. It was all I could do not to scream.

George stepped around the tent with a stick in her hands. She poked the back of the tent, rustling the fabric.

The snake turned and lashed out at the movement. I rolled backward, leaped to my feet, and took two more big steps back. Bess put her arms around me. I leaned against her, shaking, with my legs like rubber.

I took deep breaths, trying to calm down. George came around to join us, her face pale and glistening with sweat. I slowly turned my head back toward the tent. I had to force myself to look at the snake again. I imagined it lunging at me, then pushed the thought away.

I cleared my throat. "Suggestions?" My voice sounded funny.

We all stared at the snake. George said without enthusiasm, "On the wildlife TV shows sometimes they use a forked stick. . . ."

"I'm not going near that thing," Bess said firmly. "We get Kyle. He's in charge; he can deal with the snake."

Felix was tidying up his cooking gear, so we asked him which one was Kyle's tent. The flap was open, and when we called his name, Kyle sat up yawning. "Do you need something?"

"Advice," George said. "How do you get a rattle-snake out of a tent?"

Kyle frowned as if pondering a riddle. "How do you—" His eyes popped open. "What? Do you mean—are you serious?"

I managed a smile. "Sorry to disturb you, but we could use some help."

"Yes, sure." He crawled out and stood up. "You're sure it's a rattler?"

"Well, it was rattling," I said. Just the memory of the sound made me shiver.

Kyle nodded. "We'd better get Tom." He collected Tom and they borrowed one of the giant plastic tubs Felix used for food storage. Back at our tent, they peered inside.

"Boy, that's a rattler all right," Kyle said. "A big one too."

"It's a beauty," Tom said.

George whispered, "A beauty?" and rolled her eyes.

"Well, thank goodness it wasn't an ugly one," I muttered.

Tom put the tub on its side against the tent entrance. "Rattlers like dark, enclosed spaces. If we annoy it, it will go into the tub for safety."

Kyle peered through a side vent to keep an eye on the snake. Tom went to the back of the tent and pounded his hands against the nylon.

"Nothing yet," Kyle said. "He's just hunkered down."

Tom grabbed the tent poles and started shaking the tent.

"Why don't you just dump the tent out?" George asked.

"We don't want your gear to go into the tub with the snake," Tom answered.

"Good plan," Bess whispered.

Tom shook the tent and stomped his feet for a couple of minutes. Finally Kyle called out, "He's moving! He's heading for the tub. . . . Just another foot . . . He's in!"

Kyle and Tom rushed around the sides of the tent and flipped up the tub. They peered inside. "Boy, it's not happy," Tom said. We could hear it moving and rattling, but didn't get close enough to watch.

"Let's put him in the Land Rover, and I'll drive him a couple miles away," Kyle said. He picked up

54

one end of the tub and Tom grabbed the other. "Sorry about this," Kyle added. "We've never had a snake in camp before."

"It was probably just looking for shade," Tom added. "Make sure you keep your tent flap zipped when you're gone. That should prevent any more nasty surprises." They headed off to the Land Rover.

I looked at my friends. "Does anyone think that snake got in there by itself?"

Bess shook her head. George said, "No way. That tent flap was zipped." She tipped her head to one side. "Tom sure was good with the snake. You could tell he'd handled them before."

"He knew what he was doing, all right," I said. "But would he let us see his expertise if he was responsible?"

"He couldn't refuse when Kyle asked him to help," Bess pointed out. "That would have made Kyle suspicious. Kyle didn't seem fazed by the snake either. Maybe they find snakes all the time on these digs." She shuddered.

I frowned. "Tom was at the dig all morning."

"He might have slipped away for a few minutes during lunch," George suggested. "And don't forget about Jimmy. He had all morning to prowl around here, and if he lives out here, he's probably used to snakes and knows where to find them."

"Other people here might be good with snakes too." I sighed. "We have a lot of work to do. But I have to lie down for a few minutes. I still feel all jittery."

"Me too." Bess glared into the tent. "I'm trying to forget that the snake was on *my* sleeping bag."

"You know, maybe we should check the insides of our bags, just to be safe," George said. Bess moaned. We picked up our sleeping bags, held them at arm's length, and shook them out. Then just to be sure, we felt them from bottom to top, checking for lumps.

Finally we all settled down. George adjusted the tent flaps for maximum airflow. I lay back and took deep breaths to relax my jangled nerves. "Don't let me fall asleep," I said.

George yawned. "No way."

"How could we sleep after that?" Bess mumbled.

All right, I guess I slept. That's the only way I can explain the dream. Cartoon dinosaurs hid behind our tent, asking for help. Tom turned into a snake and hissed at me. I awoke with a gasp.

"What?" George mumbled. She sat up, yawning and blinking. "Shoot," she said. "I should've set an alarm."

Bess sighed and rubbed her eyes. "I needed that."

I guess I did too. Oh well, a long afternoon nap meant it would be easier to stay awake at night. That's probably when anything would happen.

We joined the others and hiked back to the dig site. It still felt hot, but at least the sun was at an angle so you could find shade.

As we neared the site, I heard a strange noise. A kind of chugging rumble. At first I thought it was thunder, but it was too long and steady. "Hear that?" I asked.

George frowned. "Some kind of car?"

Bess had the answer, of course. "Sounds like an ATV—an all-terrain vehicle."

"You mean we have visitors out here?"

Kyle picked up speed. George, Bess, and I hurried after him.

As we broke out into the hollow, I saw the ATV parked up on the cliff ahead. Then I saw the two men standing over the rock that had been damaged.

Kyle charged toward them like a bull. "What are you doing?" he bellowed.

7

Twin Troublemakers

The men looked up with friendly smiles and stepped toward us. They must have been around twenty. Both had blond hair and strangely light gray eyes. They were tall, lean, and good-looking. It took me a minute to decide that they weren't actually twins, although they had to be brothers. One was a bit taller and broader, with an air of leadership, so I guessed he was older.

Something struck me as familiar about them, but I knew I'd never seen them before. Maybe it was just seeing the two of them, so much alike, that gave that sense of déjà vu.

The first one said, "Hi! I hope we're not disturbing anything. We were just looking around."

"How did you find us?" Kyle demanded.

The guy kept his friendly grin. "We didn't. You found us. We wondered where the people were."

"I mean how did you find this site?"

He gestured toward the ATV. "We were just tooling around in our little buggy and saw this stuff. We wondered what you could possibly be doing, out here in the middle of the desert."

Kyle crossed his arms. "That's my question exactly. You know this is federal land."

The stranger kept smiling. "Yes, and I know it's legal for me to be here. This area isn't restricted."

"It may be legal," Kyle admitted, "but it's still a bad idea. Off-road vehicles cause erosion, damage the vegetation, and disturb the wildlife."

The guy shrugged. "You're entitled to your opinion too."

The younger brother hadn't spoken yet. He just watched everything with those pale eyes. The rest of the volunteers had gathered around us and were listening to the exchange. Bess sauntered toward the ATV. She stood at the base of the cliff and looked up at it.

The younger brother walked over to her and they spoke for a minute. Then he led her toward the end of the hollow, and helped her scramble up a path to the top of the cliff. A minute later she was examining the vehicle.

I knew Bess was doing her best to find out everything she could about the vehicle. George, meanwhile, had pulled out her digital camera and was casually taking a few pictures. I turned my attention back to the first brother, who was asking about the fossils. Kyle still looked unhappy, but I guess he couldn't do much. He had no real reason to think that these men were thieves.

The older brother crouched and examined the bones Russell and George had partially uncovered. "How do you know what's what?" he asked. "I mean, how do you know when you've found something valuable?"

"Experience," Kyle said brusquely. "And we're not treasure hunters. We're looking for scientific evidence."

The young man looked up and grinned. "Sure. I meant valuable to scientists. Who else would care about a bunch of old bones?"

Kyle's expression almost made me laugh. Finally he said, "That's right. They're not much use to anyone else. No value at all. But we should get back to our pointless work. And I'm sure you have other things to do."

This time the guy took the hint. "I guess so. Thanks." He gave a cheerful wave and joined his brother by their vehicle. Bess exchanged a few laughing words with him, then headed back down the path. Kyle watched them all solemnly. The ATV backed up and pulled away in a cloud of dust.

When Bess joined us, Kyle hissed, "Did you see anything in their car? Anything that might be a fossil?"

"No," Bess said. "They have a toolbox in the back, but I couldn't get a look inside it. I'll know the tire tracks, though, if I see them again."

Kyle's eyes widened. I suppressed a chuckle. Guys are always fooled by Bess's girly exterior. It's fun to watch when they realize that there's a sharp mechanical mind inside the pretty, model-like exterior.

George was oblivious to the exchange of smiles. She stepped up to Kyle and said, "So, can we switch places? I'm ready to try something different."

Kyle looked around, noticing for the first time that everyone had been waiting and watching him for the last ten minutes. He took off his hat and ran his hands through his hair. "Right. Let's see what needs to be done."

He started at the damaged fossil, where Steffi and Grayson had been plastering. He crouched, poked at the plaster, and then bent to look under the edge. "Nice work, you guys. This one's ready for flipping. Let's do that first, so everyone can watch."

He looked around. "Where's Abby?" She had disappeared. Kyle frowned. "Didn't she come back with us after lunch?"

"I'm sure she did," I said. I'd checked for every-one.

"Maybe she forgot something and went back," Bess said.

"She worked on this, so I don't want her to miss it," Kyle said. "We'll give her a few minutes. But I want to get the other side plastered today."

He stood and looked at the other fossils under excavation. He deemed Russell and George's ready for plastering.

Tom and I hadn't been quite so successful. Kyle pointed out areas between the bones where we could remove more rock. Plus, he wanted us to go a little deeper into the ground. "This leg bone is going to be thick. We'll want to dig down at least six inches underneath it."

I paced restlessly. How could I stay interested in bones when I had a mystery to solve?

Bess sidled over to me. "What's up?"

"I want to look for clues, but I'm not even sure what kind of clues to look for." I gazed around the hollow. "What kind of clues would a fossil thief leave behind?"

"If it's Tom, probably nothing. Since he's supposed to be here, footprints or dropped items don't mean anything."

"True. But what about tire tracks?" I took a deep breath. "All right, here's our first question. Did the thief take the fossil away on foot or in a vehicle?"

Bess frowned. "I thought it had to be by foot, but now that I've seen that ATV out here . . ."

"Tom said jacketed fossils weigh fifty pounds and up. That sounds like a lot to me, but he said they carry the lighter ones out in backpacks. The piece of the fossil that broke off probably wasn't that heavy, but they may have hoped to get the whole thing. Either way, it would be easier to use a vehicle. We know now that an ATV can drive up from just about anywhere. Let's look for tire tracks all around the rim."

"People will wonder what we're doing."

I shrugged. "Judging by the snake, I'd say someone already knows we're investigating."

We scrambled up the path Bess had used before, and we looked at the tracks left by the two young men. "Kyle was right; those ATVs do tear up the landscape," I said. "And this dry ground would show the tracks for days."

"There's more than one turn, but they may have circled around a couple of times for fun," Bess said. "Heading out from here, it looks like just one set out and one back, but if they drove over the same path, you might not see the older tracks."

"So nothing definite, unfortunately."

We scrambled down into the streambed to complete the circle. "No more tracks," I said. "Unless they parked farther away and walked the last part."

"Look, here comes Abby." Bess pointed. Abby was hurrying down the streambed from the direction of camp. We climbed down the cliff edge to meet her.

"What are you doing?" she snapped.

I stared at her, wondering why she suddenly seemed so rude. "Um . . . just looking around."

"Kyle has been waiting for you," Bess said.

"I had to go to the bathroom," Abby mumbled. She pushed past us.

Bess and I raised our eyebrows at each other. "What got into her?" Bess whispered.

I glanced at my watch. "Abby was gone more than twenty minutes. Maybe she isn't feeling well."

"She wouldn't have had time to go back to camp, so she couldn't have been there."

I shrugged and we went back to the group.

Kyle looked up as Abby approached. "Oh, there you are," he said. "Good. Let's get this jacket turned over."

He grabbed a long pry bar and slid it into the gap beneath the jacket. He glanced at Grayson and Abby. "I hope you don't mind if I take over now?"

"Please," Grayson said. "I wouldn't want to be responsible."

Abby just nodded. She seemed distracted, or maybe she really was sick.

Kyle worked carefully, wriggling the pry bar and moving it to different spots. There definitely seemed to be an art to the whole thing. The plastered fossil broke free with a crack, and the audience cheered. Steffi jumped forward with a small cargo net and laid it next to the jacket. "All right, let's get the muscle in here."

Kyle and Tom crouched next to her. Kyle counted off "One . . . two . . . THREE!" and with a collective grunt the three of them turned over the jacket so it lay on the cargo net.

We all stepped closer to see. The underside mostly looked like rough rock. Kyle grinned. "Great job with the excavation. There's hardly anything exposed on this side. This will make a real treasure for the museum." Kyle's expression darkened suddenly. "If we can get it there," he muttered. He stood up. "All right. Let's finish the jacket. We need to take away a little more rock, to make it lighter, but not much—this fossil is delicate. Then we can get this side plastered." He addressed Abby and Grayson. "Do you two feel like working on it more?"

They agreed, and Steffi got them started.

"Now what should we do with the rest of you?" Kyle asked.

"I'm ready to try some excavating," Bess said.

"And I wouldn't mind jacketing," George said.

Tom broke in. "I'd like to scout around a bit. See what else is out here."

"All right," Kyle said. "Russell? Do you want to keep working where you are, or do something different?"

"I could use a break," he said. "How about I take over Tom's fossil and start the jacketing?"

Kyle nodded. "Sounds good. That means George can help you with the plaster. Bess, you can work on this other one. Nancy, what do you want to do?"

"Is it all right if I go along with Tom? I'd like to get an overview of the area." And keep an eye on him.

"Sure, whatever you want," Kyle said.

I pretended I didn't notice Tom's scowl as I said, "I'm ready when you are."

"Wait!" George said.

I turned back quickly. "What's wrong?"

George pulled out her water bottle. "Better drink before you go."

I grinned and did as she suggested. Then I followed Tom to a pile of tools. He picked up a hammer with a curved head and said, "Might as well grab yourself a rock hammer. I'm not just going for a walk; I want to do some real work out there."

I opened my eyes wide. "Of course. I'm ready to help."

I took one last look around the hollow to make sure everyone was at work. Abby and Grayson had started chiseling at the underside of the fossil. Kyle was showing Bess how to use a small chisel. Steffi was explaining to George and Russell how to paint the exposed fossil with glue, to strengthen the bone, before jacketing. With Tom, that was everyone.

I trotted after Tom as he strode out of the hollow.

We went up the dry streambed. The width varied from five to fifteen feet. The sides were mostly taller than my head. Tom slowed down and started looking more closely at the rock walls.

"What exactly are you looking for?" I asked.

"Anything interesting. It rained here last week. We sometimes get an inch or two of rain in an hour. It pours into these channels—arroyos, they call them here—and suddenly you'll have several feet of rushing water. Those flash floods can wash away some of the rock and expose new fossils. I'd like to find another area like that hollow."

"So you might see fossils right up on the surface of the ground?"

"Sure. Or sometimes bones sticking out of the wall."

We moved down the streambed. It got wider, and some of the rock changed. "See this dark fine-grained rock?" Tom said. "That's mudstone. Mud settled here millions of years ago and eventually compressed into rock. It's a great place to find impressions."

"Um, impressions of what?"

"Well, leaves for one thing." He pointed at a design on a smooth, flat piece of rock.

I leaned closer. Sure enough, you could see the delicate veins of a leaf. "Wow! You mean that was really an ancient leaf?"

"Not quite. The leaf didn't turn to rock, the way dinosaur bones turned to rock. Instead, the leaf left its imprint in the mud. The leaf decayed, but the impression stayed. More mud covered up the top."

He picked up a large rock that was layered like a stack of cardboard. Tom tapped the rock with his hammer, and some of the layers peeled off. "Every flood put down a new layer of mud," Tom said. "Each layer turned to stone. Sometimes you find imprints between the layers. Plants are most common, but you can also find dinosaur footprints."

"Now, that would be cool."

He grinned at me. "Absolutely. Dinosaur footprints are actually pretty common. But it's still exciting to find some."

"Would I even recognize them?"

He shrugged. "Depends. Sometimes it's obvious that you have something unusual. But imagine that you have a huge, heavy dinosaur walking in the mud.

The footprints are going to be smeared. You might wind up with a vague impression of the heel and three toes."

"So what should I do?"

"Look around, and call me if you find anything odd."

Tom took one side of the streambed, and I took the other. He moved a lot faster than I did. I guess he could just glance around and spot something interesting. I had to look closely. In the next hour I called him over to examine two actual leaf prints, and maybe a dozen things that weren't anything. Calling him to look at my finds kept him from getting too far ahead. I started to believe Tom really was just looking for another fossil site. He didn't seem like he was hurrying to meet anyone or get anywhere.

I crouched to examine something strange. A slab of stone stuck out from the sandy ground at an angle. Three curved grooves on the stone were half-hidden by the sand.

I brushed some of the sand away. The grooves were close together and pretty deep. It looked like someone had scratched through mud with a pencil. I didn't think it was a footprint, and it certainly wasn't a leaf impression, but I didn't know what it might be.

"Tom?" I looked around. I didn't see Tom anywhere. He must have gotten ahead.

I didn't want to leave; I was afraid I wouldn't be able to find the scratches again. I cupped my hands around my mouth and hollered, "Tom!"

The desert was eerily silent. No, not silent—for the first time I noticed a low buzz that seemed to vibrate through the air. Insects, no doubt, though I couldn't tell what kind or where they were. The sound seemed to be all around me, like something out of a horror movie.

A scuffling noise broke through the buzzing. Something on the cliff above me?

What kind of animals had Steffi mentioned? I ducked closer to the cliff wall to stay out of sight. I considered calling out for Tom again but decided to stay quiet. It hit me that I was alone in the desert, a mile or more from the dig site. What if the criminals were out there and had gotten Tom? What if the criminal was Tom?

Something moved above my head. I gasped and looked up.

A cascade of rocks tumbled toward me.

8

No Claws for Alarm

Dust and pebbles rained onto my face. I leaped back.

A piece of the cliff fell away and crashed to the ground right where I had been standing. Large rocks tumbled past my legs, while smaller shards bounced and hit me in the arms and face.

I stumbled on the rough ground and sat down hard. I scooted backward as rocks clattered and bounced. Dust billowed up in plumes of gray, making me cough.

Finally the noise stopped. I looked up to the top of the cliff.

Tom stared down at me. "Nancy! Are you all right?"

I stood and backed farther away from the cliff.

My heart was racing and I had a few scratches on my arms, but otherwise I felt okay. "I'm fine," I said shakily.

"Thank goodness. I'm sorry. I didn't realize the edge was so loose."

I brushed myself off and then squinted up at Tom. "How did you get up there?"

He gestured farther along the streambed. "You can climb up a little way ahead. I wanted to get higher so I could see landmarks. Then I heard you call out, so I came running."

"You didn't have to hurry," I said. "I just wanted to show you something."

"Hang on, then, and I'll come back down."

He trotted off along the cliff top. I stepped closer to examine the rock. I could see where the top edge had crumbled away.

Had he been trying to hurt me? If I hadn't jumped back in time, I could be lying under that pile of rocks. I remembered the close call with the snake, and shivered. Someone was trying to scare me, or get rid of me altogether. I'd have to watch my step with Tom, until I figured out if this was an accident or another attack.

He joined me, wiping sweat from his face with a bandanna. "I'm really sorry about that. You're sure you're not hurt?"

"Mostly just dirty," I said.

He grinned. "You and me both."

I looked at his dusty jeans. "Did you fall too?"

"When the rock gave way under my foot, I fell backward." He held out his hands, which were scraped and bleeding. "But I guess it was better than falling over the cliff."

"Definitely," I said, "but you should still clean those scrapes. Here, let me get some water."

I pulled out my water bottle and splashed some over his hands. "Thanks," he said, drying them on the bandanna. "Now, what did you want to show me?"

"Oh, right. We'll have to clear away some of these rocks." We rolled the biggest boulder out of the way and tossed aside some smaller rocks. I kept glancing up at the cliff, but it stayed in place. Finally I uncovered the scratch marks. "Are these anything interesting?"

He crouched next to me. "Hey, this is great!" He dug at the sandy ground until he had exposed the bottom of the scratches. "These are claw drag marks."

"Oh?"

"Imagine a giant lizard, with long claws." He held out his hand, with the three middle finger hooked like claws. "When it takes a step, the foot drags back, leaving claw marks." He demonstrated, dragging his hand across the sand and leaving three grooves.

I tried to imagine a giant lizard walking through the streambed, dragging its feet and leaving claw marks for me to find millions of years later. I smiled. "So, can you tell what made them? Was it a dinosaur?"

"Probably not an actual dinosaur, but maybe a phytosaur. That was an early version of a crocodile. They lived in the Triassic, but mostly in the water, while the dinosaurs were on land." He grinned at me. "It's still an excellent find. Let's see what else we have here."

We scraped around in the sand, looking for anything similar. We found a few more claw marks. Then Tom swept some debris off of a flat rock and exposed a long, twisting mark. He sat back on his heels and frowned at it for a minute. "I've never seen one in the Triassic before, but I think this might be a tail mark. The museum would definitely want to collect that."

"That's great," I said. "I feel like a real paleontologist."

Tom stood and craned his neck to see out of the streambed. "We'd better head back now. The sun is getting pretty low. Just let me mark our location." He punched some buttons on his GPS and then we headed for the dig. This time we stayed together and walked quickly, without looking for fossils.

"I'm glad you came with me," Tom said. "At first I thought I'd cover more ground on my own. But you definitely did more than your fair share. Thanks for all your help!"

"After finding this, will you be leading the next dig?" I asked.

Tom grinned. "Could be. First I'll probably come out with one of my professors to take a closer look. If the site looks promising, we may do a real dig."

"Maybe you'll find one of those important fossils, like the one that was damaged," I hinted. "That would get you started on the road to fame, right?"

He shrugged. "That fossil is important if you're a paleontologist. Most people have never heard of a Coelophysis, so it's not really big news."

"But I thought it was valuable."

"Oh, sure. It would fetch thousands from a museum, maybe even more from the right collector. But it's no *Tyrannosaurus rex* to excite the public. Anyway, it's not my specialty. I'm more interested in those marks you found."

"You mean your specialty is footprints? I thought paleontologists were all pretty much the same."

He laughed at my surprise. "You'd be amazed at how specialized we get. People become experts on specific dinosaurs, certain types of prehistoric plants, or even on coprolite—fossil dung. Even that gets preserved and studied!"

Tom was fading from my suspect list. His motive didn't seem so good after all. And despite his skill with snakes, and the accident at the cliff, he seemed like a nice enough guy. My instincts told me he was all right—which meant I was on the wrong track.

It took only fifteen minutes to retrace our steps. Bess and George were still at work. Tom paused to talk to Kyle. I crossed the clearing and put the rock hammer back with the other tools.

I turned to study the clearing. Everybody was still there, and seemed caught up in their work. How could I make the best use of my time?

I called George and Bess to join me for a water break. We gathered out of earshot of the others.

"So, how was your hike with Tom?" Bess asked.

I told them about the rock fall and the claw drag marks. "I'm starting to believe Tom is all right, though I can't be one hundred percent sure."

"The jury is out on this whole bunch," George said. "They're all suspects, as far as I can see."

I took off my hat and ran my fingers through my hair. "So, what are we going to do next?"

"Drink more water, for one thing," George said.

She peered into Bess's face. "Are you all right?"

Bess's skin glistened with sweat. She looked droopy—and Bess never looks droopy.

"I have a headache," Bess said. "It's just the heat. I've been drinking, really I have. But it's so hot out here."

"Maybe you should rest for a while," I said.

George nodded. "You don't want to get heatstroke. Keep cool, and keep drinking, but just a little at a time. We should have brought out a sports drink, for the salt and electrolytes."

"Why don't you go back to camp?" I said. "Have a cold drink, and sit in the shade."

"One of us should walk back with you, in case you feel faint," George said.

Bess smiled. "How about I ask Kyle to take me back? I can pump him for information on the way."

George and I laughed. "I guess you're not feeling too bad," I said. "All right, see if you can get your handsome escort."

When Kyle saw how Bess looked, he quickly agreed to walk back with her. "It's time to stop, anyway," he said. "Hey, everyone! Let's start cleaning up. I'm sure Felix will be waiting for us."

Kyle and Bess started back for camp, while the rest of us put away tools and made sure everything was secure for the night. I took a long look at the valuable fossil. It couldn't be moved yet, because the plaster was still damp. But now that it was out of the ground and completely covered, it was more a target for thieves than ever.

I turned to George. "I have a hunch this is going to be an interesting night."

9

Laws and Outlaws

Nobody talked much on the way back. I tried to strike up a conversation with Steffi, hoping I could lead it around to Jimmy, but she gave only one-word answers. Everyone looked hot and tired.

A surprise awaited us at camp. Erlinda was there, talking to Kyle. George and I grabbed sodas from the cooler, then joined Bess in the shade.

"What's up?" I asked.

"It's like watching a play," Bess said. "Erlinda was talking to Felix when we got here. She's being really friendly now. She even started asking Kyle all these questions about fossils. How valuable they are, where you find them, things like that. And Kyle is trying hard not to tell her anything useful!"

"Poor Kyle," I said. "He must think everyone is out to get his fossils."

George smirked. "Speaking of poor Kyle, how was your walk back?"

"Fine. He's really nice."

I could tell from Bess's tone that she no longer saw him as a hunky potential date. She went on. "It's not just this dig that is getting him down. He and Steffi are together—they're getting married soon. But they can't afford a down payment on a house on his salary and her graduate student stipend. He's afraid they'll be in a tiny apartment forever."

That explained why Bess was no longer interested in Kyle. She'd never try to steal another girl's boyfriend. "That's too bad," I said. "Unfortunately, it also gives Kyle and Steffi a motive for stealing the fossil, if they need the money."

Bess shook her head. "I just can't believe they would do something like that. I spent a lot of time with Steffi today. She works hard, and I'm sure she's honest. Kyle is a sweetheart too. I like them both."

"I do too, actually," I said. "They seem nice, and so sincere about their work."

"I like them," George said. "But don't forget that scene at Steffi's tent last night."

I sighed. "That's right. It seems like whenever I'm ready to decide someone can't be a suspect, I remember something that says they still are. We need to investigate Jimmy, anyway. He's our number one suspect now."

"So what is Erlinda doing here?" George asked. "If she and Jimmy are involved in the fossil theft, isn't she just calling attention to herself?"

Erlinda walked past us without glancing our way. I called out to her. "Hello, Erlinda. How's Jimmy?"

She turned and glared at me. "You leave him alone! I don't need any more snooty city girls giving him bad ideas." She stormed off, following the road back toward her house.

"Okaaay . . . ," George said. "I think we can forget about getting a dinner invitation."

Bess's forehead wrinkled. "Is her behavior suspicious, or is she just unfriendly?"

"She's up to something now," I said, "but she's not a good candidate for last night's theft. That would be fast work, if she learned that fossils are valuable only yesterday evening. Could Jimmy be the thief, and his mother doesn't know it?"

George grinned. "Sounds like we get a field trip to the ranch tonight."

Felix called us to dinner—an enormous pot of chili, plus a long loaf of garlic bread. We all ate like we hadn't been fed in days. It's amazing how hungry you get working outside—or solving mysteries.

I called across the fire to Kyle. "So, what did Erlinda want anyway?"

"She wants to find a million-dollar fossil on her land. But like most Western ranchers, she only owns a small fraction of the land her cattle use. She leases the rest from the state." He gave a wry smile. "Of course, most ranchers think of all the land they use as 'theirs,' even if it isn't legally. In any case, the land she owns is higher. It's not the same geologic era as our spot, unfortunately for her."

"She must be annoyed at that," I said. "Do you think she'd try to dig here?"

Kyle's smile turned to a scowl. "I don't know. But so far, she doesn't know enough to do any damage. She hardly knows what a fossil looks like, and I certainly wasn't helping her."

"She couldn't legally dig here, right?" I asked. "What exactly is the law?"

"Basically, you can't take vertebrate fossils from government land. That means dinosaurs, mammals, and anything else with a backbone. It's considered stealing government property."

"But it's legal to dig on private land, isn't it?" George said. "Why don't people just do that?"

"First of all, in these Western states, the federal government owns a lot of the wild land, and obviously you can't do much in cities or suburbs," Kyle said. "Second, ranchers who have a lot of fossils on their land know they're worth money. They might charge thousands of dollars to let someone dig, and take a percentage of whatever is found."

Steffi broke in. "Once you take a bone out of the ground, no one can tell where it came from. So why would you pay a lot of money, if you can just sneak in and take the fossils for free?"

"Um, maybe because you're honest?" George said.

Steffi smiled. "Sometimes people don't even know they're committing a crime. You wouldn't believe the people who get caught doing illegal digs! Graduate students, school groups, scouting troops, youth groups. Hey, it's fun and educational!" She shook her head. "I guess they just don't think."

Kyle nodded. "Anyone might pick up a bone or two while they're out on a hike. It's still illegal, and it can cause trouble if we want to excavate that site. Maybe you would have had a whole skeleton, but now you have only part of it. It does damage."

He turned and glared in the direction of the dig. "But the professional thieves are the real problem. One study found that about a third of all fossil sites in Western grasslands showed signs of poaching."

After one day on a dig, stealing fossils seemed like a lot of work. "And people can really make enough money to make it worthwhile?"

Grayson broke in. "A few years back, thieves dug up a site in Badlands National Park. They got eighteen skulls worth five thousand dollars each. Some kind of rhinoceros, right?"

Kyle nodded. "They were titanothere skulls. A mammal sort of like a rhinoceros. Thirty million years old."

"A museum at the University of Michigan also lost some rhino fossils," Grayson added. "The thieves actually took apart the exhibit, took a skull and a leg bone, and then put the case back together."

Abby shook her head and made a tsking sound. "Such foolish human vanity. The pure of spirit know that fortune is merely a distraction in the search for truth."

Russell snorted. "Is that why you're here? You think you'll find some kind of truth?"

"What does truth look like, Abby?" Grayson asked. "Will you point it out to me when you find it? Maybe I can take some home. I can always use a little more truth."

I could tell they were teasing her, but she took it seriously. "One must put aside the self, and open oneself to the divine guidance of spiritual beings. We have lessons to learn in this life."

Russell rolled his eyes. "What lessons do you get from a dinosaur dig?"

84

"Positive creative activity is part of our work to heal ourselves, each other, and mother earth."

George leaned over to me and whispered, "So long as the activity doesn't involve any heavy lifting."

Felix served brownies for dessert, then we helped clean. I was tying up a garbage bag when George waved Bess and me away from the others. "Someone is hiding behind that truck," George said. "I saw movement, but he ducked back. It's not someone from camp. I counted everyone."

"Great work," I said. "Let's spread out and see if we can get another look. He was behind that blue SUV?"

"Right," George said. "That's Russell's, but he's building up the campfire."

We split up and walked casually around the clearing. I didn't look at the SUV directly but kept it in the edge of my vision.

A head bobbed up. I kept walking slowly, not directly toward him. He lifted a hand for a second, then ducked back down.

I changed direction and joined George. "It's Jimmy. His mother comes here openly, but he sneaks around. Interesting. I don't think he knows I saw him."

"So now what?" George said as Bess came over. "Wait—there he goes. Do we follow?"

"Of course!"

We wanted to give him a head start, so he wouldn't know we were following. That's when we saw someone else start down the road.

"What's Steffi doing?" I murmured.

"It looks like she's following Jimmy," George said.

"It could be a coincidence," Bess said. "Her tent's over there."

Steffi paused and looked toward camp. We could see her through the SUV windows, but I doubt she could tell we were watching. She gave the campsite a long look, then hurried after Jimmy.

George, Bess, and I exchanged curious glances, then followed. Jimmy was already out of sight. If Steffi just went to her tent, we could hurry ahead and try to pick up his trail.

We darted between low trees and bushes. Steffi hurried straight for her tent, without glancing back.

"See?" Bess whispered. "She's probably just getting her jacket or something."

"Wait!" I hissed. "Not such a coincidence after all."

Jimmy stood up from behind the tent. Steffi greeted him without surprise. She unzipped her tent and the two ducked inside.

"Let's go closer," I said. "I want to know what they're saying." I pointed to the top of the rock outcropping next to the tent and we crept up the side.

We stretched out on top and looked down at Steffi's

tent. We were only about ten feet away, but if they came out, we could duck back. Unfortunately, we could hear only snatches of conversation.

"You don't know my mother," Jimmy said.

"Forget about her," Steffi said. "You have to do this—for you."

"You know I want to, more than anything."

Their voices dropped, and I heard only a few words. A couple of minutes later, they crawled out of the tent. Jimmy held a brown paper bag. I wished I had X-ray vision and could look inside!

"Just keep those hidden, and it will be all right," Steffi said. "I'll see you tomorrow."

Jimmy nodded and scurried off toward his house. Steffi strode back to camp.

"That was interesting," I whispered. "I just wish I knew what it meant."

"Could it be a romance?" George asked.

"No way," Bess said promptly. "She wouldn't choose Jimmy over Kyle."

"You wouldn't," I said. "But that doesn't mean no one would."

Bess looked worried. "Do you think we should tell Kyle?"

"No. Not yet, anyway. If it is a romance, it's none of our business. If they're involved with the fossil theft, that's different. But we need proof." I glanced at Steffi as she disappeared back toward camp. "Come on," I said, "let's take a walk. It's time we found out more about Jimmy."

George looked at her watch. "We have about half an hour until sunset, and then half an hour of dusk until it's really dark. Should we get our lights?"

I hesitated. "I'd rather not go back to camp, and maybe attract attention. The moon will still be nearly full."

Walking along the road was easier than driving had been, and we made good time. I was just glad we had on long-sleeved shirts and pants. They gave us some protection against the mosquitoes that were starting to attack.

The crickets began chirping and somewhere an owl hooted. Something darted past our heads. I watched the small dark shape flying erratically. "Just a bat, going after the mosquitoes."

"We need a flock of them," George said, waving her hands around her face. "I'll take one for each shoulder as bug guards."

After we'd gone about a mile, George pointed. "There—I see lights." As we got closer, we could see a house.

"It's still light out," Bess said. "Do you think they'll see us?"

"If we want to see what they're doing, we can't wait too long," I said. "I'll bet ranchers go to bed early. At least the windows aren't facing directly this way. But let's keep that barn, or whatever it is, between us and the house as long as we can."

We left the road and cut across the desert. The sunset reached all around the horizon. In the west the sun was sinking below the distant mountains in a blaze of pink and gold. The few wispy clouds looked like glowing cotton candy. In the east the distant hills glowed a rosy red.

An eerie howl pierced the air. My skin prickled. Bess jumped and said, "What was that? A coyote?"

"Relax," George said gruffly, though I noticed her glancing all around. "Coyotes don't attack people, remember? Your average pet dog is probably more dangerous."

Bess nodded, but moved closer. She gasped when another bat flew past. I think we all felt better when we reached the barn. Even if it wasn't actually safer, it felt more familiar and civilized.

"We'll have to sneak around toward the house now," I whispered. "Keep close to the barn. We're less likely to be spotted."

I led the way to the corner and peered around at the house about a hundred feet away. I studied the windows, looking for any sign of movement. Everything seemed still.

I glanced back at Bess and George. "Get ready to run for it." They nodded.

I stepped around the corner of the barn. A door swung open in my face.

I stifled a gasp and pressed myself against the wall. Jimmy stepped out of the barn and pushed the door closed behind him. I was only a few feet away; he would spot me with a glance.

He trotted toward the house without turning his head. I held my breath and listened to my heart pound. I was afraid he would look back at any moment, but I was afraid to move, too, in case I attracted his attention. Finally he went through the door, calling out, "Ma!"

I slumped back against the wood for a moment. "That was close," Bess whispered.

I nodded and took a deep breath. "At least now we know where Jimmy is, and it sounds like his mother is inside too."

"But we don't know if Jimmy has brothers and sisters," Bess said. "And what about his father?"

"We'll have to risk it," I said, "but it might be better if we don't all go up to the house. Why don't you two search the barn. If Jimmy has been stealing fossils, maybe he's hiding them in there."

When they had closed the barn door behind them, I dashed toward the house. I tiptoed along the wall. Through one window I saw a small bedroom with shabby furniture. The next room was probably Jimmy's. Men's clothes lay across the bed, and farm equipment catalogs covered the desk.

I glanced through the next window at the kitchen. Erlinda was washing dishes at the sink. A flickering glow from the next room suggested a TV. I pressed against the wall out of sight and listened.

Several minutes passed with no noise besides the splashing of water, the clinking of dishes, and the murmur of the TV. The air had cooled rapidly with the sun going down, and I shivered. I glanced at the barn, a darker shape in the gathering dusk, and wondered how Bess and George were doing. It would be even darker inside the barn, and they wouldn't want to risk turning on a light.

Finally I heard a creak and Jimmy's voice. "All right, Ma, I'm going to look at the new issue of *Ranch and Range* before bed."

Erlinda grunted and Jimmy's steps moved away. I slid back along the house to Jimmy's window and peeked in. Jimmy was backing out of the closet with a brown paper parcel in his hands. The same one Steffi had given him?

He took a step toward his door, opened it, and

looked down the hallway. Then he closed the door, sat at the desk, and started unwrapping the parcel. It was a grocery bag folded over and taped down. Jimmy withdrew a book.

Steffi was giving Jimmy books? That didn't seem so suspicious, but I craned my neck to read the title. Jimmy flipped it open before I could tell.

I stepped back and thought about what to do next. Then I got an eerie feeling that someone was watching me. I froze and scanned my senses, trying to figure out what sight, sound, or smell had warned me. My nose twitched. What was that musty stink?

A growl rose behind me.

I whipped around so fast I lost my balance and sat down hard. When the world stopped spinning, I looked up into a pair of yellow eyes. Sharp teeth glistened in the fading light.

Behind Closed Doors

The animal let out two loud barks. It was just a dog.

I remembered what George had said about dogs being more dangerous than coyotes. I swallowed hard and croaked, "Nice doggie."

The dog—some kind of shepherd and rottweiler mix, from the looks of it—growled again and let out a series of barks that made my eardrums throb. Its hot breath stung my eyes.

I heard the window above me slide open. "Sugar, be quiet. Sit down."

The dog sat down and whined.

"Steffi, is that you?" Jimmy whispered out the window.

Erlinda's voice came from somewhere in the house. Jimmy called out, "Yeah, Ma, I'll take a look." I tore my eyes away from the dog and looked up as Jimmy leaned out the window. "It's all right, you can get up now." He offered his hand, and I was glad to take it. My legs were shaky. He stared at me as the light from inside fell on my face. "You?"

"Nancy," I reminded him. "I'd like to talk to you for a minute."

He glanced back at the door of his room. "All right, but you'd better come in through the window." I scrambled in, and he whispered, "Stay right here."

He slipped out the door and closed it behind him. I stepped toward the desk. Jimmy had covered the book with a magazine. I lifted it and saw the book title, *Dinosaurs of the Cretaceous*. I took a quick peek in the paper bag and saw two more paleontology text-books.

Voices came down the hall. Jimmy said, "But I'm still reading it."

Erlinda answered, "I just want to get that response card."

I grabbed the dinosaur books and ducked into the closet, leaving the door open a crack so I could look out.

I heard the room door open, and saw Erlinda cross to the desk. Jimmy hovered behind her. As she flipped through the magazine, he glanced around the room. Erlinda pulled something from the magazine and walked out of my field of vision. I heard the door close.

The closet door slowly opened. Jimmy smiled at me, and looked at the book in my hands. "Thanks," he whispered. "Did Steffi send you?"

I hadn't had time to cook up a story, so I said, "No, she didn't." I took a deep breath. "Actually, I was spying on you."

Jimmy's mouth dropped open. "You—did my mother—" He glanced toward the door and lowered his voice. "She wouldn't do that. She wouldn't ask *you*."

I smiled. "Your mother will barely speak to me. No, this is about the fossil thefts at the dig. Did you know about those?"

He shook his head. "Ma doesn't like me going over there during the digs. I've hardly had a chance to talk to Steffi."

"But she gave you these books." I handed him *Dinosaurs of the Cretaceous* and he hugged it to his chest.

"I got interested in the dig last year. I want to become a paleontologist, but Ma don't hold with that. Steffi's been helping me get into college. Only, Ma will flip if she finds out. Steffi promised she wouldn't tell anyone but Kyle, just to make sure no one mentioned it to Ma."

"But your mother is interested in paleontology

now that she knows bones can be worth something," I said.

He hesitated. "She might let me volunteer on a dig to learn how to find stuff, but I want to be a real paleontologist, not just dig up things and sell them without understanding what they are. Anyway, she doesn't have the money to help pay for it." He sighed. "Steffi is amazing, but I don't know how much she can help. I don't have the money for college."

"How about a scholarship?"

He shook his head. "My grades weren't that good. I wasn't interested in school before."

I put a hand on his arm. "Keep trying. Something might turn up. I'm sorry I suspected you." I moved toward the window. "I'd better go. Is that dog all right now?"

He came to the window with me and leaned out. "Here, Sugar. This is Nancy. You be a good girl and don't give her no trouble."

I held out my hand for the dog to sniff, and swung a leg over the windowsill. "Her name is *Sugar*?" I asked.

Jimmy grinned. "She was awfully sweet as a puppy."

I smiled at him, then headed back toward the barn. As I got close, I heard a whisper. "Nancy! Over here."

I went around the corner of the barn and found

Bess and George. "Are you all right? We saw you in there!"

I quickly explained what had happened.

"So Jimmy's all right, and so is Steffi," Bess said. "I'm glad of that, anyway."

I nodded. "Unfortunately, it doesn't leave us with many suspects left. We'd better get back to camp before we miss something."

We started back toward the road. The last glow of dusk faded. "Where's that moon you promised?" Bess asked.

"I don't know. But come to think of it, the moon doesn't always rise at the same time."

"Can you believe how dark it is?" George said. "No city lights at all."

I tipped my head back and gazed up at the stars—I couldn't believe how many stars! I could actually see the sweep of the Milky Way. A shooting star flared briefly.

The air was cool and clear, and just thin enough to remind me that we were at over six thousand feet elevation. The breeze raised goose bumps on my arms, but I warmed up as we walked. We stumbled a few times in the dark, and George got a chunk of cactus stuck to her leg. Finally we made it to the road.

"Now the moon comes up," George muttered. We stopped and watched it rise, a huge pale globe. It sent long shadows along the road. Unfortunately it was behind us, so our own shadows hid the road in front of us. But eventually we made it back to camp.

Steffi called to us as we got closer. "Everything all right? We were starting to wonder about you."

"We just went for a walk," I said. "What an amazing night sky!"

We grabbed our jackets and joined the others for mugs of hot cocoa. We chatted for a while, but everyone looked tired. Abby was the first to get up. "I know it's early, but I'm wiped out. Good night, everyone." She headed to her tent.

Soon others started drifting away. George, Bess, and I went to my car. We popped the trunk, got a jug of water for rinsing, and brushed our teeth. I watched the other volunteers crawl into their tents or get things from their cars.

"Are you guys totally exhausted?" I asked Bess and George.

"Not a bit," George said.

"Actually, I feel better now that it's cooler," Bess said. "What did you have in mind?"

I grinned at my friends. "How about another moonlight stroll? I know the perfect spot."

George glanced around the camp. "We don't want to be obvious, though. We want people to think we've gone to bed."

"Good point," I said. "All right, Bess and I will crawl into the tent and make some noise. You slip away and wait for us around the first corner of the path. Then Bess can come out as if she's heading to the bathroom. I'll follow a few minutes later. If anyone notices one of us, that person will just come back and wait a little longer."

"Great," George said. "Make sure you have your hat and gloves—it's going to get colder."

The plan worked perfectly. When I slipped out, I saw lights in a couple of the tents. The moon was rising but was still low enough that I could stay to the shadows.

I joined George and Bess. They were staring toward a hill. I followed their gaze and saw a figure standing there.

"It's Russell," George said. "He's talking on his cell phone."

We listened, and sure enough, I could hear a few words drift down. I caught something about buying and selling, and the word *tomorrow*, but that was it. Then Russell pocketed his phone and headed back to camp.

We started walking toward the dig site. We had flashlights, but we didn't want to attract attention. Fortunately, we didn't need them since the path was visible, especially as the moon got higher.

I was a few feet in the lead. I glanced up at the sky, hoping for another meteor, but the moonlight was washing out the stars.

As I brought a foot forward, my ankle caught on something. I windmilled my arms but couldn't stop myself from flying forward. I landed with a grunt, sprawled out on the ground.

"Nancy!" Bess gasped. "Are you all right?"

Now the stars were in my head. I blinked a few times to clear my vision. Then I wished I hadn't. A dark, hairy shape loomed inches from my face and I heard a soft hissing.

I almost went cross-eyed trying to focus on it. The thing, as big as my outstretched hand, reared up. The moonlight shone on its furry body and thick furry legs. "Please tell me that's not a tarantula," I whispered.

"You know I don't like to lie to you," George said. "Just stay still."

The tarantula didn't move, except to bob up and down. If the movement was supposed to be intimidating, it was working. I have nothing against tarantulas—at a distance. But having one six inches from my face made me break out in a sweat.

George found a stick and nudged the tarantula away. I edged backward and sat up, catching my breath. Bess was sitting on a rock with her hands covering her face. "Is it gone?" she asked.

"That's funny," George said. "It's on a leash." I stared at her. "Look," she said. "It's attached to this string, and the string was tied around that rock."

"So maybe this was planned," I said slowly. I searched the ground. "Sure enough, here's what tripped me. Somebody strung a wire across the path."

"And left our little buddy here as an extra surprise," George said. "Nice. But what do we do about the poor thing? We can't leave it tied up." Bess moaned.

I said, "People have them as pets, right? They can't be too dangerous."

We still didn't want to take any chances. I wrapped my scarf around one glove and gently held the tarantula down. Prickles ran along my skin, but I kept telling myself it was just an innocent creature.

George worked her penknife under the string and it loosened. "Someone just dropped a noose over its head, with a slipknot," she said. "There you go, fella, all free."

We hurried away, leaving the tarantula to its own devices. We walked more carefully after that. "First a rattlesnake, and now a tarantula," George said. "Someone doesn't like us getting nosy. But are they trying to hurt us, or just scare us?"

"Maybe both," I said. "Neither creature is likely to be deadly, but a snake bite would send us out of here to find a hospital. Either the snake or the tarantula could have scared off some people. The thief seems to think we're a danger to him or her. I just wish I agreed!"

"You'll figure it out, Nancy," Bess said. "You always do."

We walked in silence from then on. When we neared the dig site, I stopped. Bess and George gathered close. "We don't want anyone to see us," I whispered. "We can scramble up the slope here. Then we can creep across the top of the bluff and look down into the site."

"We'll be more visible," George murmured, "if anyone else is up there."

I thought for a moment. "You two wait here. I'll go up slowly, and take a look around. It won't be so noticeable with just one of us, and I can crawl. If it's all clear, I'll come back for you. We can find a nice hiding spot and camp out."

They nodded. I moved carefully up the slope, trying not to dislodge any rocks that might fall and make noise. When I could peer over the top, I took a long look around. I couldn't see anyone, so I went up the rest of the way.

I stayed low, on my hands and knees. The bushes released a spicy scent, and I remembered that sagebrush grows in the desert. I had to crawl only about fifty feet, but it seemed to take forever. The sharp rocks gouged into my knees and the plants caught at my coat. One thorny branch dragged across my cheek, leaving it stinging. Did everything in the desert bite or scratch?

I crawled to the edge of the dig site and stared down, trying to see into all the shadows. Moonlight glinted on the white buckets and the smooth plaster covering the fossils, but nothing moved.

I didn't feel like crawling back across those rocks. I looked for a place where I could drop into the clearing. I moved along the cliff a few feet, to where a wide crack split the wall. I could shinny down that.

I swung my feet over the edge. A few pebbles clattered down. I froze and waited, listening for any response.

I thought I heard . . . breathing? I shook my head. Impossible. It had to be the wind, or just my imagination. I strained my ears, and couldn't catch the sound again.

I stared into the dark crevice, but nothing moved. If I kept waiting, I would trick myself into thinking I saw a face or hand, but those lighter spots had to be just paler rocks.

I took a deep breath and lowered myself into the crack. I wormed my way down until I stood hidden in the shadows. It would make a perfect hiding place. It was a little small for three people, but we could manage. We'd be hidden, and sheltered from the wind.

I took a step forward. Something rose up in front of me.

I gasped and tried to step back, but the cliff pressed in close as a pair of hands reached out for me.

11

Things That Go Bump in the Night

I opened my mouth to yell for Bess and George, but the person spoke. "Nancy? What are you doing here?"

"Kyle? Is that you?" I leaned back against the cliff, my heart pounding. "You gave me a scare. What are you doing?"

"Watching for thieves. Which brings me back to my question—what are you doing here?"

I was glad it was dark so he couldn't see the flush rising in my cheeks. I realized what he must be thinking, and hurried to explain. "Same as you. Bess and George are waiting around the corner. We wanted to keep an eye on the fossil." I grinned, though I wasn't sure if he could see that in the dark. "I was just thinking what a good hiding place this would make!"

He sighed and scratched his head. Did he believe me?

I squeezed past him. "I'd better get Bess and George. They'll be wondering what happened to me."

I quickly explained the situation as I led them back to Kyle. He stepped out where we could all see one another in the moonlight. We spoke in whispers.

"I've got things covered here," Kyle said. "I have my sleeping bag and I'm ready to spend the night. We don't all need to hang around."

"All right," I said. "We won't worry, now that we know you're here. But I wish we could find some way to help tonight."

"What's that?" George asked.

We all turned to follow her gaze. "I saw a flash of light," George said. "It looked like a flashlight."

We all stared. "There it is!" Kyle exclaimed.

"Where exactly?" Bess asked. "Oh, I saw it too! What could it be?"

I grinned at my friends. "There's one way to find out. Kyle, you'd better wait here and protect the fossil. We'll check out the light."

"Be careful. You don't want to get lost in the desert."

George patted her pocket. "I have my GPS turned on. I'm tracking our every move!"

I felt better knowing that George was keeping

track of our path. It was easy enough to follow the river channel, but if we had to chase someone across the desert, we could lose our way. George's GPS could also mark the spot if we found anything useful, like tire tracks.

We waved to Kyle and headed across the hollow, then up the path to where the ATV had parked that afternoon. We saw the light again and scurried toward it. It had to be someone with a flashlight.

We chased the light for the next half hour, getting farther away from camp and the dig. We had to go around hills, and slither down one slope of loose rocks. One good thing about the desert, we could move over the land and keep the light in sight all the time. It wasn't like a forest, where you have to fight your way through thick trees.

But the desert had its own challenges. Thorny bushes snagged at our clothes. We had to watch for cactus patches in the dim light. You could brush right past a small cactus and not realize it until you felt the thorns in your ankle.

Still, I was tingling with excitement. The cold night air, the bright moon washing out the starry sky, the scent of the desert, and most of all the chase—I felt so alive!

The light went out.

We walked for a few more minutes without seeing

the light again. I stopped and turned slowly, staring in every direction. My ears strained for any sound in the night. I heard the wind rushing past bushes, and a faint distant rumble—a train, miles away?

Bess whispered, "George, where are the night-vision goggles?"

"Yeah," George said. "That's what we need. Or at least some of those binoculars for looking at stars. They gather more light so you can use them at night."

I smiled as I imagined George back home, scheming to get new toys. But that didn't help us now.

"What should we do?" Bess whispered.

I hesitated. "Keep going, I guess. Maybe the thief dropped down into a ravine, or went around a hill."

"Or he's waiting for us there in the dark." Bess groaned.

"Either way, we can't just stand around doing nothing," George said.

We walked for another five minutes without seeing the light or anything else of interest. Finally I stopped. "There's no point in wandering around randomly. I guess we should head back."

Their shoulders drooped. We were doing a lot of hiking, and not learning much. "If someone wants to steal the fossil, why were they heading so far from the dig site?" Bess asked.

"Maybe the thieves are lost," George said.

"Or maybe they heard us with Kyle, and we scared them away from the dig." I sighed. "I think we've all had enough for tonight. Let's go back and check on Kyle. If everything is all right there, I guess we go to bed."

George nodded. Bess smiled and I knew she was relieved. She's a good sport, but after her brush with heat exhaustion earlier, she must have been beyond ready for sleep.

George pulled out her GPS. "I'll just get a reading. . . ." Her voice trailed off.

"What's the matter?" Bess asked.

George peered at the GPS and punched some buttons. She muttered something I couldn't quite catch.

"What?" Bess demanded. "What's wrong?"

George stared at the GPS, and then looked up at us with wide eyes. "There's no power. The batteries are dead!"

12

Between a Rock . . .

"You mean we're lost out here?" Bess whispered.

"I can't believe it!" George sounded outraged that technology should fail her. "I recharged the batteries right before we left." She flipped over the GPS and popped off the back. She grabbed her flashlight, turned it on, and shone it on the battery compartment. "These aren't my rechargeable batteries! Someone stole mine and replaced them. They must have put in batteries with just enough juice to turn the GPS on at the beginning, so I wouldn't notice."

We stood in silence for a minute. "What are we going to do?" Bess asked.

"We'll find our way back," I said, trying to sound confident. "We can follow our own tracks back."

George turned her flashlight to the ground. "We came that way. This won't be so hard."

She took a few steps. Her flashlight flickered and went out.

Bess moaned. "Don't tell me—bad batteries."

Bess and I checked our flashlights. Hers didn't have any batteries at all. "I put in new ones when I packed," she groaned. My light went on, but the beam looked weak. "We'd better use it only as necessary," I said.

I wondered how many miles we had walked. George's GPS could have told us, if it was working. However far we'd come already, we had that much more to get back to our tent. And going back would take much longer, since we had to move slowly.

The moon shone on silvery bushes and sent shadows between the pale rock outcroppings. As much as possible we used that light to see our tracks. Sometimes the path was obvious, because bushes or patches of cacti left only one route. When we weren't sure, we turned on the flashlight for a few seconds.

We walked in silence. The excitement had evaporated. We were lost in the desert, with no water or food. If we didn't show up by morning, Kyle would look for us. But would he know where to look? We might have covered a couple of miles, chasing after that light. Now it looked like it had all been a trick, to get us out of the way. And while we were busy being lost, the thief might have been causing more trouble.

I went over and over the clues in my mind, trying to find something useful. Every time I thought I had a suspect, the clues turned into nothing. Yet somebody had stolen those fossils!

The second flashlight went out after ten minutes. "At least I have my key chain penlight," I said. "It doesn't give much light, but it should help." I managed a smile. "And I know the thief hasn't gotten to it, because it's been with me the whole time!"

I tried to be cheerful, but my energy was fading. Bess's shoulders sagged with fatigue, and George stifled a yawn.

Fortunately, the soft desert soil showed our tracks well. In some places we could identify clear boot prints. Where the ground was sandy, we sometimes saw only shallow depressions. Then we came to an area of bare rock extending one hundred feet in every direction.

"I don't remember crossing this," Bess said.

"We must have," I said. "We just weren't paying attention on the way out."

"We'll search the edge until we find our tracks going out the other side," George said.

Bess sat on a rock, folded her arms on her knees, and put her head down. "Call me when you find it."

I glanced at George. "Maybe we all need a short break. Wait a minute—" I fished in my jacket pockets. "I have an energy bar!"

I broke it into thirds and wished again for some water. How foolish to go out into the desert, even at night, without it!

A high, quavering cry pierced the night air. The hair stood up on the back of my neck.

The howl faded in the distance. "Coyote," George muttered. "Not dangerous."

I nodded. My logical mind knew that coyotes hunted small animals and avoided humans, but some primitive part of the brain shouted, "Danger!"

Bess looked up and said in a tight voice, "I'm ready to go now." Her eyes widened as she stared over my head. She ducked back and screamed.

Something passed over my head so close that my hair moved in its breeze. Next to me George yelped. I choked on the last bite of energy bar.

My heart pounded as I watched a large bird swoop away from us. Its wingspan was as wide as my outstretched arms. "It's all right," I gasped. "Just an owl. Probably out hunting rabbits."

"Nice scream, Bess," George complained, rubbing her ear. "You just about burst my eardrums."

Bess glared at her. "Oh? It may have been loud, but I could still hear *your* scream."

"I didn't scream," George said, wide-eyed. "I maybe just exclaimed a little, in surprise."

I chuckled, the tension broken. "All right, you two, let's get out of here and back to our beds."

We walked directly across the open rock, and then scanned the edge for footprints. It might have gone faster if we'd been willing to split up, but somehow we all wanted to stick close together. I used my penlight, for speed, even though I was getting worried about that battery. The night seemed to be getting darker. I glanced up. Sure enough, the edge of a cloud bank was eating the moon.

"Here," George said, "this bush has a broken twig." We searched around it and found disturbed areas in the dirt and finally, a few feet away, a clear footprint.

"Are you sure it's one of ours?" Bess asked.

"It has to be one of ours, or the thief's," George said. "Who else would be out here?"

We looked at one another in dawning excitement. "Everyone compare your prints!" I said.

We studied our treads. The print belonged to Bess. "Oh, well," she said with a sigh. "Maybe we'll find some other good prints."

"We can't spend much time looking," I said. "We need to get back to camp, both for our sake and for Kyle's. I don't want to waste time, or the penlight battery. But try to remember what our prints look like, and if you see anything different, we'll take a closer look."

I don't know how long we walked that night. I resisted the urge to look at my watch. It seemed like hours later when Bess cleared her throat. "Um, you guys? I keep seeing these little red dots following us. I know I'm really tired, but I swear this isn't just my eyes playing tricks."

I looked around. Sure enough, I saw two small red dots off to my left. I heard a rustle like a bush moving in the breeze, and the dots disappeared.

"They look kind of like laser pointers," George murmured, looking in another direction.

We stood with our backs together and looked all around. My eyes burned with the effort of trying to see in the dark. One pair of red dots moved closer to another pair. I glanced around and saw more red dots, always in pairs a few inches apart, and about two feet above the ground.

"What are they?" Bess wailed.

"Eyes," I croaked. "Something's watching us."

13

. . . And a Hard Place

We pressed our backs together. My heart pounded in my throat. I took a deep breath and forced myself to think clearly. I tried to speak in a normal voice, but it came out as a whisper. "It must be coyotes. They've been tracking us."

"I thought coyotes didn't attack people!" Bess said.

"They probably just want to know what we're doing in their territory," I said. "Think of them like escorts. They want us out of here as much as we want to be gone."

"I have a hard time believing that," Bess muttered.

I forced myself to stand up straight and step away from my friends. "In any case, if we want to scare them off, we should look big and make noise, not huddle together and whisper."

"Open your coats," George said loudly. She unzipped hers and held it open so she looked bigger.

"Mine's a pullover," Bess wailed.

"Then wave your arms," I said.

We made ourselves as big, loud, and threatening as possible. The coyotes backed off, although we could still see the eyes glowing red at a distance. "Come on," I said. "The sooner we are out of their territory, the happier we'll all be."

We found our tracks again and walked quickly, using the penlight for speed's sake. "We should keep making noise," George said. "Anything you want to talk about?"

"There's only one subject on my mind," I said.

"Who got us into this mess?" Bess added.

"Any ideas?" George asked.

I shook my head. "I think we need a lot more information about everyone. Jimmy and Tom were our best suspects, when we knew just enough to be suspicious. But we hardly know anything about Abby, Russell, Grayson, or Felix. George, I think tomorrow you should find a spot where you can get reception and do some Internet research."

We discussed the various people on the dig, coming up with more and more ridiculous reasons to suspect them, as a way to take our minds off the coyotes.

"Russell is part of a syndicate planning a real

Jurassic Park," George suggested. "That phone call he made when we left tonight—he was calling his partners to make sure the lab is ready."

Bess laughed. "No, it's Grayson. He wants to be like those thieves he was talking about. He thinks he's Robin Hood, and he's going to give the bones to the poor."

When I could stop giggling, I said, "How about this: Abby wants a dinosaur skull as a talisman. Can't you just see her with one hanging around her neck?"

"Yeah, a big *T. rex* skull." George guffawed. "Wait, what about Felix? Maybe he wants to open a restaurant serving dinosaur soup!"

We didn't even notice when the red dots stopped following us. Finally, our tracks led us to a drop-off. I blinked several times, trying to focus my eyes and brain. Then it hit me. "We made it! We're back at the dig."

We whooped and hugged each other. As the tension drained out of me, I realized just how frightened I had been.

"Now we just have one more mile back to camp," Bess said. "I'm almost sure I can make it."

"Hold on a second," I said. "Now that we know we're safe, let's take a look for those extra footprints."

I shone the penlight around, but couldn't find

anything definite. We had our tracks going out and back. They covered up anything else.

"Maybe we can look again in the morning," Bess said pointedly.

I smiled and got up. "You're right. Let's get back to our sleeping bags."

George glanced at her watch. "Yeah. It's already two." She gave Bess a wicked grin. "Wake-up call in four hours!"

Kyle stepped out of his hiding place as we crossed the hollow. I had almost forgotten about him. We gave him a brief rundown of our adventure. After we assured him that we were okay, he explained that everything had been quiet at the dig site. Finally, we trudged the last mile back to camp.

George reached for the tent zipper, yawning. "Hold on," I said. "We don't need any more surprises tonight."

I stood to the side of the tent and slowly opened the zipper. I peered around the edge and didn't see anything dangerous. Still, we pulled our sleeping bags outside and shook them out before crawling inside. I fell asleep the second my head hit the pillow.

By the time we dragged ourselves out of our tent in the morning, we could smell the bacon and sausage sizzling. I started forward, ravenous after our exhausting night.

Bess grabbed my arm. "Nancy, at least brush your hair, please."

"Oh. All right." I quickly ran a brush through my tangles and pulled my hair into a ponytail. After two nights camping, miles of hiking, and no shower, I figured nothing much would help my appearance. George just smashed a hat onto her head.

Bess had some kind of gel that was supposed to clean your hair as you brushed it. "Try it," she said.

I grinned. "Sorry. I can't hear you over my stomach growling!"

"Hurry up," George said. "Tom and Kyle are already getting food, and I'll bet they can eat a lot."

Kyle was back? I wondered who was guarding the fossil, but first things first. George and I practically pounced on Felix.

"Smells great!" George said. "I'll take my first and second helpings right now."

Felix beamed at her and scooped a slab of omelet from an enormous cast-iron pan. "Western omelet, with onions and green peppers. There's toast on the grill, and coffee in the pot."

I pulled a chair close to Kyle. After I had a few bites of food in my stomach, I turned toward him and whispered, "Everything all right last night?"

He nodded. He had dark circles under his drooping eyelids. "You were the most exciting thing that happened. Steffi relieved me at dawn and sent me back here for breakfast. If anything had happened since then, we would have heard about it." He pulled his jacket open enough to show something that looked like a radio.

"Is that a walkie-talkie?"

"Yep. The range is good enough to reach the dig. Steffi has the other one."

I hadn't even noticed that she wasn't at breakfast. I guess hunger interferes with my observational skills. I glanced around and counted heads. Everyone else was accounted for.

Kyle took a last swig of coffee and stood up. "All right, people, this is our last full day. Let's get going so we can haul out that first jacket before it gets too hot."

We finished breakfast and loaded our backpacks with water. George whispered, "I'm going to stay behind. I'll go back up that hill where I can get Internet reception." She pulled out her handheld computer. "I'll need everyone's full name, though."

"I printed out the e-mail where Kyle listed the people coming on the dig." I rummaged through the car and found it. "Here you go."

George took it and walked off with a wave. Bess

and I started for the dig. "My feet hurt," Bess groaned. I nodded. My legs ached too, but after a few minutes of walking, the stiffness left them.

Kyle walked quickly, but his step had lost its bounce. Grayson alternately yawned and blew his nose. Abby's violet eyes had lost their sparkle, and the dark circles under them suggested she had not been sleeping well.

Russell looked awake, but caught up in his own thoughts. Out of everyone, Tom looked the most cheerful. He caught my eye and smiled.

We straggled into the dig site. Kyle stopped and looked around. "Steffi?" He took a few steps forward, frowning. "Where is she?"

A muffled grunting and scuffling came from the crack in the cliff where Kyle had been hiding the night before. I hurried toward it.

"Steffi!"

14

Secrets Revealed

A petite figure squirmed on the ground, her hands tied behind her back and her feet bound. Even with the burlap bag over her head, I recognized Steffi.

Kyle pushed past me and tugged the bag off. He gathered Steffi into his arms. "Are you all right?" he demanded.

Steffi just gasped and squirmed. I knelt behind her and examined her wrists. Rough twine went around and around them until the ends joined in a complicated knot. "Hold still," I said. "I'll get this off."

Steffi stopped squirming but she was still trembling. The knots were unbelievably tight, probably because Steffi had struggled against them so much. My fingers stung with splinters from the coarse twine.

Steffi twisted her head around. "Get these things off of me!" she croaked.

"I'm working on it." I glanced at Kyle. "Give her some water."

Someone handed him a water bottle and he held it for Steffi. She took a few swallows and started coughing. I wasn't having any luck with the knots, but I remembered my pocketknife. I slipped off my backpack, found the knife, and started sawing through the twine. Finally it came apart. Steffi's wrists were rubbed raw underneath.

Steffi brought her hands in front of her and started shaking them out as Tom freed her ankles. She hopped to her feet and paced. Everyone was asking questions, but she didn't answer. She grabbed the water bottle from Kyle and took a long drink. Finally she took a deep breath and snapped, "All right, all right! I'm fine. Just really, really mad."

"What happened?" Kyle asked.

"I heard a strange noise. A kind of tapping. I waited a minute, but no one came into view. Finally I stuck my head around the corner. Before I could see anything, that bag came down. I got in a few good kicks, but they grabbed me and tied me up."

"They?" I asked. "More than one person?"

She nodded. "Two men, I think. I didn't get a look at either of them, and they didn't speak. But one person pinned my arms while the other tied my feet. I'm pretty sure I kicked that one in the face. He grunted, or at least I think it was a man. The one holding me definitely was."

"Can you remember anything else about them?" I asked. "The one holding you, was he tall? Did he have any particular smell?"

She paused in thought. "The only thing I could smell was that nasty burlap bag. But the one holding me was definitely tall. At least as tall as Kyle, but skinnier."

Two men, one at least six feet tall and thin. "It sounds like those two guys who showed up yesterday," I said.

Kyle muttered something and turned away. "The jacket! They got our fossil."

"Of course," Steffi said. "You didn't think they went to all this trouble just for me?"

Kyle smile crookedly and took her hand. "I must admit, I actually forgot about the fossil for a minute."

She grinned up at him. "I'm okay."

Tom picked the walkie-talkie up off the ground. "So now what? What do we do?"

I looked around at the others. Everyone stared at Steffi and Kyle, looking shocked and confused.

"How long ago did this happen?" Kyle asked.

"Maybe ten minutes after you left," Steffi said.

Kyle scowled. "They must have been watching, and they waited for me to leave. We thought we were safe, once the sun came up. I can't believe it."

"They had to have had a vehicle," I said.

Steffi nodded. "I think one of them stayed here while the other went to get it. A few minutes after they tied me up, I heard the engine. Then some grunting and thumps. Then they drove off."

Bess climbed the path up the bluff, to where the off-road vehicle had parked the day before. She studied the ground and called down, "I'm sure there are new tracks here, from the same tires."

Kyle groaned. "There's no point in trying to follow them now, I guess. They have at least half an hour on us, and we're on foot." He was silent for a minute, as we all watched in sympathy.

Kyle gave a deep sigh. "All right. Priorities. Let's get these other two jackets finished. I want them out of here today, and the sooner we get the plaster on, the sooner they can dry."

It didn't take all of us to jacket two sets of fossils. Kyle and Steffi drew away to one side and talked in low voices. Grayson started helping Russell with one jacket, while Tom and Abby took the other.

I paced restlessly. It seemed like we had identified the thieves, but I still wasn't satisfied.

Bess joined me. "So, after all we went through, this is how we find out about the thieves."

I frowned and shook my head. "I'm not convinced it's that simple. Someone from camp is involved."

"What makes you so sure?"

"The snake. When it showed up in our tent, we hadn't even seen those two guys yet. Why would they try to discourage us?"

"They might have just wanted to cause trouble at camp," Bess said. "Maybe they chose a random tent and it just happened to be ours."

"Why would they want to disrupt the camp?" I said. "They wanted Kyle's group to do all the work in excavating the fossils. Otherwise they could have just come out last week, when no one was here. No, someone from camp is involved. Someone who knows I'm a detective."

"I told Abby that first morning," Bess admitted. "But I don't remember who else was around."

"Just about everybody," I said. "And of course we told Kyle later that morning. Either Abby or Kyle might have told someone else." I put my hands on my hips and looked around. "We need to find out more about these people, and we're running out of time. They don't need us here. Let's go see how George is doing with the Internet."

Bess smiled. "What's a hundred-million-year-old fossil, compared to modern snooping?"

We offered to start carrying gear back to camp. Most of the tools could go, along with the empty buckets. Kyle didn't want to expose anything new, since we wouldn't have time to get it out of the ground. I grabbed one of the walkie-talkies, too, just in case. They wouldn't need both at the dig.

We entered camp and put away the tools. George waved and came toward us. We filled her in on what had happened with Steffi. "I hope you found something interesting," I finished.

"Grayson is a lawyer," she said. "A federal prosecutor out of Denver, so it makes sense that he knows about cases of fossil theft. Nothing suspicious there. I chatted with Felix a bit, and he said he used to own a deli. That checked out. He's in his tent now with a book and a battery-operated fan. I found several guys named Russell Stevens, but unless he's a basketball player, a rock and roll drummer, or a Belgian scientist, nothing on this one. I was just going to work on Abby when I saw you come back."

"That's a good start," I said. "But we need to find out about Russell somehow. On the phone last night he said something about buying and selling. He could have been calling his helpers."

George peered through the windows of the dark SUV. "This is Russell's. Hey, his phone is on the console." George cackled and opened the door.

"What are you doing?" Bess asked, as George pushed buttons.

"Checking what number he called last. It's a 212 area code. That's New York City. Let's go up on the hill." She pushed buttons as we walked. "The magic of redial," she muttered.

"He'll be able to tell someone was messing with his phone!" Bess exclaimed.

"Only if he checks the calling record," George said, "which he won't. And even if he does, he won't know who it was." She pushed Send as we topped the hill, then held the phone to her ear and spoke. "Hello? I'm sorry, who did you say this was? Oh, I have the wrong number. Sorry."

She closed the phone. "It's a stockbroker's office."

"I guess he was just keeping track of his investments," I said.

"All right. Let me check Abby," George said. A minute later she added, "Abby's rock shop is legitimate, in Sedona, Arizona. But she doesn't just sell crystals and jewelry. She sells small fossils, too."

"Interesting," I said. "But hardly proof. All right. Let's look through her tent and car. Does anybody know which car is hers?"

"I saw Abby getting something from that silver SUV," Bess said.

It was locked. "Who locks their vehicle out here in the middle of nowhere?" George asked.

Bess rolled her eyes. "Yeah. It's not like anyone would look inside."

"It's strange, though," I said slowly. "With all her talk about nature and crystals and macrobiotic diets, I'd expect her to drive something more energy conscious, like my hybrid."

"Yeah, or an old VW Bug," George said. "But not this gas-guzzler."

I glanced at my watch. "We should have another hour before everyone gets back for lunch. George, see what else you can find on Abby. I want to look through her tent."

Bess yawned. "I'll keep watch to warn you if anyone comes back early."

Abby had a small air mattress, a sleeping bag, a bag with the usual toiletries, and a romance novel. The net pocket by the door held a good flashlight and two candy bar wrappers. She must have been keeping everything else in her locked vehicle.

I sat back on my heels and thought. Abby drove an SUV, and ate candy in her tent after eating health food in front of everyone. She had secrets. But did that mean she was the fossil thief?

I went through her tent again. This time I searched more carefully, for any tiny clue that might be hidden. I flipped through the pages of the book, but didn't see any extra scribbles. I felt the lining of the makeup bag. I even examined the attached tag, made of leather with a plastic window. Her name and address showed through.

I stared at the name. Abby Morningstar. It sounded like one of those new age last names people give themselves. I wondered what name she'd been born with.

On a hunch, I slid out the name tag. The writing on the back was faded, probably several years old. Abigail Eback.

I slid the tag back into the holder and crawled out of the tent. I waved to Bess. "Come on. Let's join George."

She looked up as we crested the hill. "Nothing new yet."

"Try looking up Abigail Eback." I explained what I'd found in Abby's tent.

A minute later George said, "I'm not getting anything on Abigail or Abby. There aren't even too many Ebacks. Let's see. . . . Wait a minute. The Arizona Reptile Zoo. Run by Darryl and Dustin Eback. They have snakes, lizards, and spiders." She frowned. "Spiders aren't reptiles."

"Those two brothers!" I exclaimed. I frowned. "I

knew there was something familiar about those two guys. I had a sense of déjà vu when we first saw them. It was their unusual eyes. Abby's are unusual too."

"It's Abby!" George said.

"It has to be," I agreed. "I'll bet those guys are her sons, and—"

"No, look." George nudged me. "It's Abby." Sure enough, she was entering camp.

15

The Fossil Escapes!

W hat's she doing back so early? Come on." I waved as I approached her. "What's up? Where are the others?"

"Still working," she said. "But I have a long drive, so I thought I'd pack up and get started. They're just hauling heavy loads today, and that's not really my thing."

"I see." My mind raced. I'd thought we'd have all day to get proof and confront Abby. But now that her sons had the fossil, she was taking off to meet them.

I snuck the walkie-talkie out of the tool pile, and dragged George and Bess behind our tent. "We have to call Kyle."

We tried, but got no answer. I finally gave up. "They must have turned off the other one." I bit my lip.

"George, run back to the dig and tell Kyle. Get help!"

She took off without a word. I hissed to Bess, "We have to stall her." We joined Abby, who had already emptied her tent. "We'll help you pack. We're not doing anything until lunchtime."

We were as slow and clumsy as we could be, but folding up a tent just doesn't take that long. We managed to annoy Abby, but she still had her SUV packed up in twenty minutes. It would take at least another twenty minutes for George to return with Kyle, even if they ran the whole way.

"Why don't you stay for lunch?" I asked Abby. "The others will be back soon."

Abby grimaced. "I can't eat all that rich food, full of meat and preservatives. I have some carrot sticks in the car. That will hold me through this afternoon."

Bess and I tried to make small talk, but Abby got into her SUV, slammed the door, and backed out.

"We have to follow her," I said.

"She'll see us," Bess said.

"We'll stay back, but we have to take that chance. Otherwise, she'll get away."

We got into my car and turned it around. Abby was already out of sight around a corner. I bounced over the rough road, going as quickly as I dared. I knew my hybrid couldn't keep up with the SUV on dirt roads, if Abby hurried.

I spotted her in the distance. "Come on, come on," I muttered, willing the car to go faster. Bess held on to the door with one hand and the dashboard with the other.

The walkie-talkie crackled. "Nancy? Come in?"

Bess grabbed it. "George? Abby took off! We're following her."

"We're on our way back. Where are you headed?"

"Toward the highway."

"We'll be right behind you."

I smiled. Now that we had backup, I was sure we could stop Abby.

A bang echoed through the car as a rock, flipped up by the wheel, hit the bottom. I jumped and clutched the steering wheel harder.

We came to a rut so deep I needed one wheel in the bushes to straddle it. I didn't have time to crawl through that area, so I just aimed and hoped for the best.

Bess squealed, "Watch out!"

The back of the car started sliding. I grappled for control.

The wheels slid into the ruts. I heard an unpleasant crunch as the underside of my car high-centered.

I winced but pressed the gas. My wheels spun. The car didn't move.

I watched the SUV disappear.

"Oh, no!" I turned off the car. "We'll never get out of here in time."

Bess sighed. "You did your best. Now what?"

I leaned my head against the steering wheel for a moment, then straightened. "We do everything we can to go after her."

I jumped out of the car and Bess followed. "If we can just push this back wheel a little to the right, we should get traction again," I said. "Good thing the hybrid is so light."

Bess perched on the edge of the driver's seat, where she could control the pedals with one foot and push with the other out on the ground. I leaned against the back corner of the car and shoved.

"All right," I called, "give it a little gas."

The wheels started to spin slowly. Dust billowed in my face.

A wheel caught, then held. The car inched forward. Bess pulled both her feet in so she could concentrate on her driving.

A minute later we were out of the rut. Bess slid over so I could get into the driver's seat. "I doubt we'll catch her now," she said.

"Our best hope is to see which way she turns on the highway," I said, easing the car forward.

"If we don't get stuck again. Wait—what's that sound?"

I listened. "An engine? We're too far to be hearing Abby."

We looked around. A dirty white pickup truck bounced across the scrubland in the distance. "It's Jimmy!" Bess cried. "Maybe he can help."

"Get out and wave." I hit the horn—three short blasts, three long ones, three short ones. Hopefully Jimmy recognized SOS.

The truck turned and bumped toward us. I eased my car to the side of the road in a wide spot and got out as Jimmy pulled up. He leaned out the window. "You stuck again?"

We ran to him. "No, but we have to follow someone." I pointed to where Abby had disappeared. "We have to find out where that SUV goes."

"Better jump in, then," he said.

Bess slid in next to him, and I jumped up beside her. Jimmy took off as we were still fumbling for our seat belts. "It's one of the women from the dig. Abby," I said. "Someone stole a fossil last night, and we think she's involved."

"That gal stole a fossil from the dig?"

"Her sons, anyway," I said. "They tied up Steffi and took the most valuable fossil."

"What!" He scowled, hunched over, and drove faster. Bess and I held on to anything we could reach.

"Steffi is all right," Bess said.

"She wouldn't like being tied up none," Jimmy muttered. In minutes we reached the highway and screeched to a stop.

I scanned the road, first left, then right. "That way!" I said, pointing toward a faint dot of silver.

Jimmy turned onto the highway. Bess spoke into the walkie-talkie. "George? We're on the highway. We turned right."

"Gotcha." Her voice crackled. "We're at camp. Be there soon."

Jimmy gained on the SUV. I hoped we wouldn't have to follow Abby all the way to Arizona. What would we do if we caught her, anyway? We didn't have proof that she was involved in the theft, just suspicions. If she was smart, the valuable fossil would never show up in her shop. She'd sell it secretly. She probably already knew interested buyers who wouldn't ask questions.

We could only wait and see what happened. A few minutes later the SUV took an exit ramp. "Duck down," I said to Bess. "Jimmy, keep her in sight. Hopefully she won't pay attention to the truck."

We followed, entering a small town. It was basically a gas station with a convenience store and diner, and a handful of scattered houses. I peered over the dashboard and saw the SUV pull around behind the store.

Jimmy parked in front. "Nothing behind there.

She must be stopping. I'll run inside and ask them to call the police."

Bess gave our location to George. We got out and crept around the side of the building. Some big garbage cans at the back gave us cover so we could see.

Abby was out of the SUV, talking to the two young blond men. The off-road vehicle sat in the bed of a cherry red pickup truck. "They figured out it was you," Abby said. "I told you it was a mistake to show up yesterday. You'd better load it into my car. If anyone stops you, we don't want them to find that fossil."

The men climbed into the bed of their truck. It would take only a couple of minutes to transfer the fossil. "We have to stall them," I whispered.

"How?" Bess asked.

Good question. There were three of them and three of us, but I didn't think we could hold them back physically. Jimmy joined us. "Tony, the convenience store owner, is calling."

"Do you think you could bring your truck around and block in their cars?" I asked.

He studied the two vehicles, parked about fifteen feet apart. "One of them, anyway. You want me to?"

"Yes. Hurry."

He took off back around the corner. The men were grunting as they lifted the heavy jacket. "Let's see if we can keep them from getting that fossil into the SUV," I said to Bess.

Abby and her sons froze as we stepped around the garbage cans. "Fancy meeting you here," I said. We stood between them and Abby's SUV.

"You again!" Abby muttered. "What are you doing here?"

"Just stopped to say hi," I said.

She turned to her sons. "Do something!"

They stood holding the jacket between them, sweat glistening on their faces. The older one grunted, "Like what? We're kind of busy here."

"Well, put that thing in the car and get these girls out of here!"

We did a kind of dance as the brothers tried to move toward the SUV, and Bess and I kept in their way. Finally Abby rushed forward and shoved Bess, who stumbled into me. As we caught our balance, Abby held out her arms to keep us back, while her sons staggered forward a few more steps.

An engine roared, and Jimmy's truck whipped around the corner. "Block the SUV!" I called, pointing. He stopped directly behind it.

The brothers groaned and started staggering back toward their vehicle. When they got close, Jimmy pulled forward so he was behind it.

I guess the boys decided to cut their losses. They

exchanged one look and dropped the jacket without a word. I winced as it hit the ground with a thud, and hoped the thick plaster coating would protect it.

"Mom, let's get out of here!" one of them yelled. They ran toward the SUV. Abby stopped trying to grapple with us and sprinted around to the driver's door. The boys tumbled into the back.

Jimmy backed up his car to block the SUV.

Abby gunned the engine and backed up anyway. Her SUV smashed into the truck bed. Metal screamed and crumpled. The SUV shoved the truck back several feet. Abby turned the wheel and pulled forward. The front corner of the SUV scraped the wall as she tried to squeeze out.

Brakes screeched as a Land Rover swung around the corner. The SUV shuddered to a stop inches away. Kyle, Steffi, and George gaped at us through the windshield.

The SUV had no more room to maneuver. For a moment no one moved. Then Abby jumped out and tried to run around Jimmy's truck. Her sons slid out of the SUV a moment later.

They were heading for the red truck, but they didn't have much chance now. I ran forward and blocked the driver's door. Jimmy jumped out and grabbed at one of the brothers, while Bess planted herself in front of the other one.

George, Kyle, and Steffi joined us. A man came out of the store and called in a Spanish accent, "The police are coming! You need help?"

We had them surrounded. Abby glared at us. Her older son glanced around wildly, as if looking for an escape. The younger son gave up first. With a sigh, he turned and placed his hands on the car, his feet spread. He acted as though he had been arrested before.

Sirens sounded in the distance, then grew louder. A police car pulled around the corner. An officer jumped out and Jimmy quickly explained the situation. They got Abby and her sons in a line along the side of the truck. Another police car pulled up before the first officer had finished reading their rights.

"Thanks for your help," Kyle said as we watched. "How did you connect Abby to those men?"

I grinned and explained about our research. I turned to Abby as a police officer led her to his car. "Did you legally change your name to Morningstar?"

She scowled, and then relented. "I guess you'll find out. Eback was my married name. When I divorced, I changed to Morningstar."

"And all that stuff about organic food and nature spirits?" George asked. "That was all an act?"

Abby shrugged. "It helps sell crystals and jewelry. Besides, I figured no one on the dig would suspect me if they thought I was that kind of nut. But the real money is in rare fossils. One good Internet deal, and I make more money than the store makes in a year."

"Did you tell your sons to put the snake in our tent?" I asked.

She sneered. "I did that myself. Who do you think taught them to handle snakes and spiders? They spotted the coyote den when they were out driving yesterday, but I was the one who led you to it." She sighed. "Obviously, it didn't do any good."

Abby joined her sons in the back of the police car, and the officer drove off. The other officer got into his car and spent several minutes on the radio. Kyle crouched over the fossil. He examined it, then let out a sigh of relief. "The jacket looks all right!" He grinned up at us. "I can't tell you how glad I am that you all came on this dig."

We helped Kyle get the fossil into the back of the Land Rover. Tony brought out an armload of sodas and passed them around, demanding the details of the story.

The second police officer got out of his car. "Looks like the Feds will be involved in this one. Oh, by the way—there's a ten-thousand-dollar reward for this capture. I guess you girls get it."

George gasped. I could almost see her counting off the things she could buy with her share. Then I saw Kyle put his arm around Steffi and pull her close. Jimmy was telling Tony about his part in the capture. He looked proud, but when he gestured toward his crumpled truck, he sighed.

I looked at George and Bess. George groaned. "We're not going to get any of the money, are we?"

"Just think," Bess said. "Jimmy could fix his truck and get started at college. Kyle and Steffi could put the money toward a down payment on a house. What do we need that compares to that?"

George sighed and nodded.

"I've had an adventure," I said. "You couldn't buy that with any amount of money. It sounds to me like a happy ending all around."

Kyle called over to us. "Are you ready to go back to the dig? I don't think Jimmy's truck is going anywhere, but he can come back with us. We still have a couple of jackets to haul out this afternoon, after lunch."

"Lunch," George said. "Now *that* sounds like a happy ending."

Think Nancy's done solving crimes?
Think again!
Read ahead to get a sneak peek
of the first book in the new Nancy Drew trilogy:

Pageant Perfect Crime

Is it my birthday?" my friend Bess asked, fluffing her hair in the rearview mirror as she slid into the passenger seat of my car. "Do you owe me a favor? Or is it just my lucky day?"

I smiled as I pulled the car back into the street. "Bess, what are you talking about?"

"How many times does *Nancy Drew* call me up and say she wants to go shopping? I'll tell you how many times: never."

"Bess, come on." But I couldn't help smiling a little: Bess was right. She's always decked out in the latest fashions; I'm happy if my pants match my shirt. When Bess talks to me about clothes, she usually has to stop and explain what a "bubble skirt" or an "empire waist" is.

"Let me guess," Bess went on, pausing to turn to

me with a mischievous grin that showed her dimples. "You don't *really* want to go shopping. I'm betting you have an ulterior motive. A little snooping to do? Some questions to ask?"

I shook my head and pretended to sigh. "Oh, Bess, you know me too well."

"I was surprised you even knew what Fleur *was*."

I nodded. "Have you shopped there before?"

"Actually I just heard about it." Bess reached into her purse and pulled out a fashion magazine. "*Pose* magazine says it has the best espadrilles for summer. But I never heard a word about it before—you know, before the big scandal."

My mouth dropped open. "You know about the scandal?"

"With Miss Pretty Face and the shoplifting? Sure. Nancy, where have you been?"

I shrugged. I was beginning to wonder how I'd missed out on the River Heights Scandal of the Year myself. "I guess . . . snooping?"

Bess laughed. "I guess. Seriously, you should make more time to watch the local news. Or at least *Extra*." She pointed to a small, neatly landscaped minimall on the right. "I think it's in here, way in the back."

I pulled in and we drove around for awhile before I realized what Bess meant: *way* in the back, hidden on the other side of the building. Finally, I parked in front of Fleur, a handsome store with two big display windows filled with mannequins in sparkling cocktail dresses.

"So what are you investigating now?" Bess asked, shoving the magazine back into her purse. "A shoplifting ring? A credit card scam? Is Fleur unwittingly selling counterfeit purses or jewelry?"

I shook my head. "Believe it or not, it's the scandal you mentioned."

"Miss Pretty Face?" Bess looked surprised. "Portia Leoni?"

I nodded.

"I thought that was over and done with," Bess said. "She did it. They caught it on tape. End of story, right?"

I shook my head again. "It's not that simple. She says she had an agreement with the store to borrow the dresses for free publicity. But after she picked them up, the shop owner changed her story. She thinks someone set her up. And if I don't find out who, she might lose her scholarship and have to leave the university."

"Hmmmm." Bess stared at the display window, thoughtful. "Well, if anyone can get to the bottom of this, it's you, Nancy."

Inside, Fleur was abuzz with activity. Business women swished skirts off display racks, high school kids tried on accessories, and an angry mob surrounded the espadrilles, all fighting to grab the ones featured in Bess's magazine. Bess split off to join the mob as I walked around, getting the lay of the land. I had to admit, a lot of the clothes they carried were really cute. But I *never* would have found this place if Bess hadn't known where to go.

Near the counter, a middle-aged woman with short auburn hair was helping an older woman match a bracelet to a cocktail dress. "We just got these in last week," she said, holding a jet bracelet up to a red-and-black beaded dress. "I wasn't sure when I ordered them, but in person, they're absolutely gorgeous."

Aha, I thought. If she'd ordered merchandise for the store, she had to be the shop owner, my target.

I lingered around the counter while the older woman bought the dress and bracelet. Then I sauntered over. "Good morning," I said warmly.

"Good morning," the shop owner responded, giving me the once-over. Her voice cooled a bit when she saw my outfit of worn T-shirt and khakis. "I'm Candy. Can I help you with something?"

"I hope so," I said, smiling. "I actually have some questions."

She nodded. "Need help with sizes?"

"Not really," I said, and leaned closer. "I was actually

wondering about an incident that happened here. A shoplifting incident. With—"

But Candy's face had already changed, closing off completely. "If you're asking about the Miss Pretty Face scandal, I've already discussed that matter with the police."

I decided to try a different tactic. "Actually, I work for the university bookstore," I lied, "and Ms. Leoni just applied for a position with us. I told her we couldn't possibly hire a shoplifter, but she had a different version of what happened here. She says she was *told* to pick up the dresses by someone from the pageant, and that you seemed to know about that when she came by to get them. Perhaps there was some kind of misunderstanding?" I raised my eyebrows hopefully.

But Candy was having none of this. "Portia Leoni is a liar," she whispered fiercely, looking around the store to see if anyone was watching. "The camera doesn't lie, Ms.—"

"Drew," I supplied.

Candy nodded. "Ms. Drew. I'm not going to discuss this any further. What reason could I possibly have to lie about a theft in my own store?" She looked up at me, but I caught something strange in her expression. Nervousness—almost as though, deep down, she was worried I *might* know a reason she would lie.

"Nobody's calling you a liar," I said carefully. "I just—"

"Good day," Candy spat, and abruptly turned away to approach another customer. "May I help you find a size, Miss?"

I stood at the counter for a moment, stunned. *Wow. She* really *doesn't want to talk about it,* I thought. Here's something funny about people who are telling the truth: They'll talk about anything. Embarrassing incidents, controversies, whatever. A person who's telling the truth has nothing to hide. Liars, on the other hand—they'll avoid the subject at all costs. And half the time, they'll try to make *you* feel bad for bringing it up.

I had a pretty strong suspicion which category Candy fell into.

I wandered over to find Bess, who was eyeing a butter-colored leather handbag while she chatted with a sales clerk.

". . . one hundred percent leather," the sales clerk was saying. "And if you feel it, you can tell it's of the highest quality."

Bess sighed, running her fingers over the purse's surface. "It *is* beautiful," she agreed. "It's just a little outside my price range. Do you think it might go on sale soon?"

The sales clerk—her nametag said 'Dahlia'—shook her head, looking apologetic. "Probably not," she advised with a little shrug of her shoulders. "Business has been so busy lately. We haven't had a sale since . . . well, since before that Miss Pretty Face thing."

Hmmmm. I leaned in.

"So business picked up after that?" Bess prompted.

Dahlia nodded. "Oh yeah, tons. It went from being dead in here to being packed, all the time. In fact"— she glanced over at Candy, saw that she was still busy helping the woman she'd left me for, and lowered her voice—"it's kind of weird, but before the shoplifting? We were told the store might close at the end of the month. With this lousy location, we couldn't get any customers."

Bess turned to meet my eye. I could tell she knew I was putting something together.

"Hmmm," she said, stroking the purse one last time. "Well, thanks for your help, Dahlia. I'm going to pass on the purse today. But congrats on the great business—I'll have to come back and check out your new stock next week."

Dahlia smiled, took the purse back, and then turned to help another customer. I gave Bess a little nod, and we strolled out of the store and back to my car and climbed in. Still thinking it over, I turned the key in the ignition.

"So," said Bess with an expectant look, "any help-ful info?"

I nodded slowly. "The owner sticks to her story,

that it was a shoplifting," I said. "But there's something off about her. She seemed tense—like she had something to hide."

Bess nodded. "And what Dahlia said?" she asked. "About the store almost closing? I could see all the gears turning in your mind."

I smiled. "It's odd, isn't it? The store was losing money until Portia supposedly shoplifted, and then all of a sudden business was booming."

"What do you think it means?" Bess asked.

I sighed. "Maybe someone paid Fleur's owner to accuse Portia of shoplifting," I replied. "If they were losing money and the store was about to close, that makes them ripe for a bribe."

"Hmmm." Bess reached out and tapped her fingers on the dash. "So what are you going to do?"

"I don't know," I admitted. "It's possible that someone *did* set Portia up. But who, and why? And how can I even figure out the answers to any of these questions when I know nothing about the pageant itself?"

I drove a bit, and suddenly became aware of a change in Bess's expression. She was staring at me, grinning. When I turned and looked at her at a stoplight, she looked like she was about to explode—like Christmas, her birthday, and a half-off sale at Macy's had all arrived on the same day, right then.

"*Nancy,*" she said. "You know what you have to do?"

I shook my head. "What?"

Bess bounced up and down in her seat, fishing a pamphlet out of her purse. "You have to compete for Miss Pretty Face!"

She handed me the pamphlet. In the few seconds before the light changed, I read:

Are you the next Miss Pretty Face River Heights? All young women aged 16–18 are invited to join our pageant! Compete for scholarships, endorsements, and the opportunity to represent the best in your generation!

"You have got," I said, pulling away as the light changed, "to be kidding."

"Nancy, it's perfect! You qualify, and you're adorable! Plus it would get you right into the middle of things—meeting all the pageant bigwigs, figuring out who had the most to gain!"

I bit my lip.

"You *know* it makes sense," Bess argued. "I could help you, be your fashion coach. I'm sure George would help too. It's a great opportunity! Maybe you'd even win!"

I shuddered. "Nancy Drew, Pageant Girl?"

Bess rolled her eyes. "Don't be a snob, Nancy. Come on."

I sighed, pulling up to Bess's house. I'm about the least pageanty person in the universe. I hardly ever wear makeup, and I doubt "snooping" counts toward the talent competition. I tried to picture myself up on a stage—huge hair, sparkly dress, blinding smile, crying demurely as a tiara was placed on my head.

Not that I'd *ever* win.

I looked at Bess, who was looking at me with that excited, expectant look. If this was Christmas morning, I had become Bess's Santa Claus.

"All right," I said, covering my ears to block out Bess's shriek of joy. "I'll do it."